Business End of a Six-Gun . . .

"You're under arrest," Longarm said. "Now shuck that gunbelt and turn around with your hands behind your back. We'll all take a nice little ride and I'll send you back to Cheyenne direc'ly."

The shooter did not have sense enough to leave a bad situation alone. He had to make it worse.

He went for his gun.

It was the last mistake he would ever make.

Longarm's hand flashed and his Colt belched lead, flame, and smoke.

The .45 bucked in Longarm's hand once, twice, a third time.

The gunman was driven backward with each shot. Then his legs buckled and he pitched forward, facedown in the dirt beneath his feet.

"I wish you hadn't done that," Longarm muttered.

"What the hell is going on back there?" the jehu shouted.

"Just taking care of business," Longarm said.

DON'T MISS THESE
ALL-ACTION WESTERN SERIES
FROM THE BERKLEY PUBLISHING GROUP

THE GUNSMITH by J. R. Roberts
Clint Adams was a legend among lawmen, outlaws, and ladies. They called him . . . the Gunsmith.

LONGARM by Tabor Evans
The popular long-running series about Deputy U.S. Marshal Custis Long—his life, his loves, his fight for justice.

SLOCUM by Jake Logan
Today's longest-running action Western. John Slocum rides a deadly trail of hot blood and cold steel.

BUSHWHACKERS by B. J. Lanagan
An action-packed series by the creators of Longarm! The rousing adventures of the most brutal gang of cutthroats ever assembled—Quantrill's Raiders.

DIAMONDBACK by Guy Brewer
Dex Yancey is Diamondback, a Southern gentleman turned con man when his brother cheats him out of the family fortune. Ladies love him. Gamblers hate him. But nobody pulls one over on Dex . . .

WILDGUN by Jack Hanson
The blazing adventures of mountain man Will Barlow— from the creators of Longarm!

TEXAS TRACKER by Tom Calhoun
J.T. Law: the most relentless—and dangerous—manhunter in all Texas. Where sheriffs and posses fail, he's the best man to bring in the most vicious outlaws—for a price.

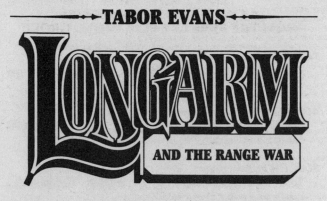

--►► **TABOR EVANS** ◄◄--

LONGARM

AND THE RANGE WAR

J

JOVE BOOKS, NEW YORK

THE BERKLEY PUBLISHING GROUP
Published by the Penguin Group
Penguin Group (USA) Inc.
375 Hudson Street, New York, New York 10014, USA
Penguin Group (Canada), 90 Eglinton Avenue East, Suite 700, Toronto, Ontario M4P 2Y3, Canada
(a division of Pearson Penguin Canada Inc.)
Penguin Books Ltd., 80 Strand, London WC2R 0RL, England
Penguin Group Ireland, 25 St. Stephen's Green, Dublin 2, Ireland (a division of Penguin Books Ltd.)
Penguin Group (Australia), 250 Camberwell Road, Camberwell, Victoria 3124, Australia
(a division of Pearson Australia Group Pty. Ltd.)
Penguin Books India Pvt. Ltd., 11 Community Centre, Panchsheel Park, New Delhi—110 017, India
Penguin Group (NZ), 67 Apollo Drive, Rosedale, Auckland 0632, New Zealand
(a division of Pearson New Zealand Ltd.)
Penguin Books (South Africa) (Pty.) Ltd., 24 Sturdee Avenue, Rosebank, Johannesburg 2196,
South Africa

Penguin Books Ltd., Registered Offices: 80 Strand, London WC2R 0RL, England

This is a work of fiction. Names, characters, places, and incidents either are the product of the author's imagination or are used fictitiously, and any resemblance to actual persons, living or dead, business establishments, events, or locales is entirely coincidental

LONGARM AND THE RANGE WAR

A Jove Book / published by arrangement with the author

PRINTING HISTORY
Jove edition / January 2012

Copyright © 2012 by Penguin Group (USA) Inc.
Cover illustration by Milo Sinovcic.

ISBN: 978-0-515-15028-5

JOVE®
Jove Books are published by The Berkley Publishing Group,
a division of Penguin Group (USA) Inc.,
375 Hudson Street, New York, New York 10014.
JOVE® is a registered trademark of Penguin Group (USA) Inc.
The "J" design is a trademark of Penguin Group (USA) Inc.

PRINTED IN THE UNITED STATES OF AMERICA

10   9   8   7   6   5   4   3   2   1

Chapter 1

Deputy United States Marshal Custis Long stepped around behind Marshal William Vail's broad desk and pulled the roller blind down about halfway, peered back at his boss for a moment, and tugged it about six inches lower.

The United States marshal for the Department of Justice's Denver District watched Longarm throughout this odd sequence, then spun around in his swivel chair to follow Longarm until his best deputy had resumed his seat with a grunt and a nod.

"Mind if I ask what that was all about?" Vail inquired.

"The light, Billy."

"What about the light?"

"It was reflectin' off your pate."

"My *pate*?"

"Right. Pate. It's—"

"Dammit, Long, I know what a pate is."

"Right. Well the light was shinin' off yours. Got in my eyes. That kinda hurt, you see an' . . ."

Billy Vail, it was true, was bald as a hard-boiled egg. In fact he looked as innocent as a cherub, with his pink com-

plexion and round face. The truth was that he was as hard-
boiled as any of his deputies and more so than most, having
come up in the lawing business first as a town constable,
then a town marshal, and later a Texas Ranger. A good one
too by all accounts. Now he sat behind a desk in a comfortable chair and issued orders to other men with one hand,
while dealing politics with the other. Custis Long, better
known as Longarm to friend and foe alike, would not have
traded places with Billy for love or money.

"Shut up, Long. I didn't call you in here to tell me
jokes."

"Bein' blinded ain't no joke, Billy. Why, I recollect a
time—"

"Will you please be quiet and listen to me?"

Longarm took the hint—a rather broad hint—and clammed
up. He crossed his long legs, reached inside his coat for a
slender, dark brown cheroot, and proceeded to prepare it to
smoke. He nipped the twist off with his teeth and spat the
bit of tobacco into his palm, then struck a Lucifer on his
boot sole before carefully lighting the cheroot.

While Longarm was so occupied, Billy Vail explained,
"I got a wire this morning from Sheriff John Tyler of
McConnell County, Wyoming Territory. Do you know it?"

"I know the county. It's prett' nigh due north from here,
almost to Montana. I been through there a time or two.
Don't know any Sheriff Tyler, though. He any kin?"

"Kin to whom?"

"President Tyler, of course."

"Dammit, Long . . ."

"Sorry, Billy. I'm just in a good mood, that's all." He
had won almost fifty dollars playing poker the previous
evening and felt rather good about that.

Vail shook his head. "Sometimes, Custis, I think I like
you better when you're in a shitty humor."

Custis. The boss had called him Custis. Longarm knew that was a sure sign that he better straighten up and be quiet. So thinking, he physically straightened himself on the office chair, planting both boots on the floor and holding the smoldering cheroot down at lap level. "Yes, sir. Sorry."

"The problem in Dwyer . . . Before you ask, Dwyer is the county seat up there . . ."

Longarm indeed had already known that, but he had no intention of speaking up to say so.

"The problem is a range war that seems to be developing among the stockmen in McConnell County."

"Sheepmen and cattlemen, I suppose," Longarm drawled, smoothing the ends of his dark brown handlebar mustache.

"Actually, smart aleck, it is *not* along the normal lines of these things. This time it is between sheepmen and goat-herds."

"Goatherds? You're shitting me," Longarm said, his eyes going wide and his jaw dropping just the least little bit.

"It sounds like that, I know, but according to Tyler they are deadly serious about this. I don't know the specifics, but the man's wire, brief though it is, claims there could be blood shed by the bucketful if something isn't done, and he just is not capable of doing it. He did not say why, but he makes it clear he is powerless to stop the war."

"Any idea how many are involved in this thing?" Longarm asked.

"No idea, but it must be serious for him to call on us."

Longarm leaned back and stared at the ceiling in deep thought, then dropped his chin and looked at the boss again. "There's no train up that way so's I'd best take the night train to Cheyenne an' a stagecoach north from there."

"Good. Henry can give you travel vouchers, of course."

"Uh, one thing, Boss."

"Yes?"

"Who's going with me?"

"Do you see anybody else in this room, Custis?"

"No, sir."

"That's right. The reason you don't is that I have no one else to send with you. You'll have to do this on your own."

"Shit, Boss, I was hoping for some backup this time. Besides, I thought it was just you Texas Ranger boys that had the 'one riot, one Ranger' policy. When did we go an' adopt that?"

"When the attorney general asked me to take charge of this office." Billy snorted, then stood and gathered some papers out of his top drawer. "Now if you will excuse me, the district attorney and Don Fenster are waiting upstairs to chew me out."

"If you don't mind, Boss, I'll stay down here and get that stuff from Henry." He grinned. "Though you know that otherwise I'd be right in that room with you, telling those boys how wrong they are to be chewing on your ass."

"Yeah. Sure." Billy grabbed his hat on the way out, leaving Longarm to amble out into the front office, where the marshal's chief clerk was laboring over some paperwork.

"Reckon you know what I'm here for," he said.

The slender, bespectacled Henry pointed to a sheaf of already prepared vouchers with one hand while with the other he shuffled through a side drawer in search of something else.

Longarm picked up the offered forms, folded them lengthwise, and tucked them into an inside coat pocket. He retrieved his dark brown Stetson from a hat rack and headed out into the city, a tall, weather-beaten man wearing black stovepipe boots, striped corduroy trousers, a brown tweed coat . . . and a very large six-gun in a cross-draw rig at his waist.

Chapter 2

Longarm tugged his Ingersoll railroad-grade watch from his vest pocket—the other end of that same watch chain was attached to a custom-made .41-caliber derringer—and checked the time. He had, if memory served, a good five and a half hours before the northbound left for Cheyenne. That should be plenty of time.

He practically skipped down the stone steps of the Federal Building, turned left at the corner near the U.S. Mint, and hailed a cab.

"Where to, mister?" the hack driver asked. His horse tossed its head, throwing a stream of slobber in Longarm's direction. Longarm ducked out of the way, and the wet goo landed on the back of a passing woman's dress. Under other circumstances Longarm might have stopped her and offered to pay for the dress to be cleaned. But, as he was in a bit of a hurry, he ignored the little problem and crawled into the cab, giving the address of his boardinghouse on the other side of Cherry Creek as he did so.

"Yes, sir, right away."

When the cab pulled up beside the picket fence at the

front of the boardinghouse, Longarm bounced out with a wave and a called "Be right back."

"Hey!" the cabbie protested, but by then Longarm was hurrying up the steps to the porch and inside.

He went upstairs and grabbed his carpetbag—always packed and ready, down to and including a full bottle of Maryland rye whiskey—plus his McClellan saddle, bridle, Winchester, and saddlebags.

"I'll be back," he called over his shoulder to his long-suffering landlady on his way out.

"Now where?" the cabbie asked, obviously not in such a fine humor about this fare now.

"The Glass Palace," Longarm said as he climbed inside the cab again.

"Don't even think about walking off like that when we get there," the hack driver warned.

"Wouldn't dream of it," Longarm assured him, settling back onto the cracked oilcloth upholstery.

The driver snapped his whip above the horse's ears and the cab lurched forward. Twenty minutes later it came to a halt outside Jim Burnette's Glass Palace.

"Dollar twenty," the cabbie called down from his perch high above the front wheels. It should have been a fifty-cent ride at most and both of them knew it.

"Ain't that a mite high?" Longarm countered.

"That's the fare. Pay it or I'll call a cop."

"But I *am* a cop," Longarm said.

"And I'm the queen of fucking England. Now pay the fare, mister."

"Right." Longarm dug into his pockets and produced a dollar and a half, which he handed to the fuming cabbie. "Keep the change," he said as he turned and headed for the alley beside the run-down theater.

The cabbie gaped in disbelief and Longarm snickered

quietly to himself. That would teach the SOB to not be so quick to judge, he thought.

He walked through the trash-strewn alley to the stage door, almost all the way back on the left.

He had to set his carpetbag down in order to have a hand free to knock twice, pause, and knock once more. Seconds later the door opened a mere crack and an eyeball peered out at him. A split second after that the door was swung fully open.

"Nice t' see you this afternoon, Marse Long."

"Nice t' see you too, Cleofus. Is she in?"

"In her dressin' room. Here, let me take them things. They be safe with me."

"I know they will, Clee." He passed his burdens across to the porter, stagehand, all-around help inside the theater.

"Should I announce you, Marse Long?"

"No, I'll surprise her if that's all right."

"It be fine with me. You go on now. You know the way."

Longarm grinned and poked Cleofus playfully in the ribs. The old black man countered with a make-believe right cross to Longarm's jaw. Cleofus used to be a professional pugilist and likely could still hold his own. He and Longarm were friends of long standing.

He headed around behind the curtained back of the stage, ducked under some guy wires and through some large, painted muslin scenery panels to the three dressing rooms on the far side of the theater.

Longarm went to the farthest of the three and paused there. He was smiling when he pushed the door open without knocking.

There before him, reclining on a red velvet fainting couch, was perhaps the prettiest girl in Denver. Or anyway, in his admittedly prejudiced opinion, the prettiest at this moment.

He tiptoed toward her, unbuttoning on the way.

Chapter 3

Marthabelle Whitcomb was resting between shows. She was made up in the broadly vivid and overdone makeup required for the stage, and her hair was hidden behind a wrap of brown butcher paper so it would not be disarranged when she lay back against the upholstery. She was wearing a loose silk chemise, a garter belt, and thigh-high black stockings. And nothing else, as was quite apparent.

Longarm took a moment to simply look at her. Lovely. It seemed a damn shame that such fine bones and pale, wonderful complexion should be hidden beneath layers of rice powder and garish rouge.

Nothing could hide that figure though. Long, slender legs. Narrow waist. Firm swell of breasts surmounted by tiny, rose-hued nipples.

Her bush, blond and luxuriant, peeped out beneath the hem of her chemise.

Silently chortling, Longarm wakened the girl by dipping a fingertip beneath that bush and into the soft, rubbery slit he found there.

Marthabelle's sky blue eyes snapped open. There was a

moment of hesitation as she came back from sleep. Then she smiled. "Bastard," she whispered.

"Bitch," he responded.

"You stood me up last night."

He shrugged. "I was busy." He had been playing cards but knew better than to offer that as an excuse. He was not going to lie to her either, although he could have claimed some urgent mission connected with his work. Marthabelle would have believed him, but Longarm was not fond of lies or of liars. "So I came tonight."

He bent down to kiss her, but Marthabelle rolled her face to the side. "Don't. You'll muss my makeup and it takes forever to put on."

"What does all that stuff feel like?"

"Like crap, actually. It's like wearing a mask. Ugh!"

Longarm settled for lifting the hem of her chemise and kissing her nipples, one by one and back again.

"Oh, my. It's a shame we don't have more time. Come to think of it, what time is it?"

Longarm produced his Ingersoll and told her.

"The maid will be here to help me into my costume in twenty-five minutes."

He grinned. "That's plenty of time."

"You can't, love. It would ruin my hairdo even if you didn't touch the makeup."

"Goodness, the things you women go through to make yourselves beautiful for us men. Stand up."

"What?"

"Up. Get your pretty ass off that couch."

"Why?"

"Just do it."

Marthabelle stood, a questioning look lifting her eyebrows and putting a faint crease into the greasepaint and powder on her forehead.

"Now turn around," Longarm said, taking her by the shoulders and turning her to face the couch. "Bend." He gave her a gentle push, bending her over.

"Oh, no," she said.

"Oh, yes."

"There isn't time."

"If you say so." By then his fingers had slipped between the cheeks of her ass to again find and fondle the opening to her pussy.

Longarm knew the girl. Knew her responses. He laughed. "You're already so wet you're damn near dripping your juices on the floor. It's a wonder it ain't running down your legs. An' right pretty legs they are, if I do say."

"Custis. No." But Marthabelle's body betrayed her words as she wriggled her butt and moved back onto his probing touch. "Really, dear. The time."

"Shh." His cock was out, standing tall and hard as stone. He pressed a hand between her shoulder blades to push her a little lower. With his other hand he spread the cheeks of her ass, and crouching, he positioned the head of his cock at the entrance to Marthabelle's pussy.

A slow shove, a tiny bit of resistance, and then her body opened itself to him.

Longarm slid full-length into the sweet, wet heat.

Marthabelle moaned softly and pushed back against him so as to take him deeper inside herself. "Oh," she muttered. "So big."

"D'you mind?"

"I love it. You know I do. Hush now, dear. Pay attention to what you are doing."

Longarm laughed a little. And set about finishing what he had just started.

After all, the maid would be coming in twenty-five minutes. He figured to be coming a little sooner than that.

Chapter 4

"What time is the next stage to Dwyer?"

The stage line clerk looked up from his newspaper and said, "Eleven o'clock." Longarm already had his watch in hand before the clerk added, "Tomorrow."

"Say what?"

Newspaper still in hand, the clerk said, "We have northbounds rolling out Monday, Wednesday, and Friday, southbounds coming back Tuesday, Thursday, and Saturday. Nothing going nor coming on that route on Sundays. This here being a Tuesday . . ."

"Right. I get the picture. Tomorrow." Longarm thought for a moment, then asked, "If you have an overnight turnaround for that coach, why d'you start so late in the day? Why not early morning?"

"That's for the mail. Our contract calls for us to carry mail headed that way, and we don't get the pouch until the overnight mail has got here and been sorted. So we wait until we have that ready to go."

"That explains it, thanks. Can I leave some of my gear here until that coach is ready then?"

"Sure. Just set it inside the cage here. Nobody will bother it."

"Thanks. I'll be back tomorrow morning."

The clerk nodded and went back to his reading. Longarm deposited his saddle, saddlebags, and rifle inside the office portion of the stage depot but kept his carpetbag with him while he went in search of a room.

That requirement was satisfied easily enough, and within half an hour he was out on the streets of Cheyenne with a day to kill and no duties to fulfill until he caught that northbound coach in the morning.

He found a saloon that had provided pleasant diversions in the past and dropped in.

The bartender nodded and said, "Rye whiskey, isn't it, friend?"

"You have a good memory," Longarm said. "Yes, it'll be rye."

"Bottle or glass."

"Just a glass." He dug into his pocket and laid a quarter down. The barman dropped the coin into his apron pocket and slid a bowl of peanuts down the bar to Longarm before pouring a generous measure of excellent rye and placing that next to the peanuts.

Longarm picked up the glass and inhaled the bitingly sharp aroma of the whiskey before tasting it. He nodded to the bartender appreciatively and swallowed a good third of the rye, then reached for a peanut roasted in the shell.

He was on his second whiskey and probably twentieth peanut when he heard a commotion in the street outside. There were shouts, then gunshots. Two in quick succession followed by a brief pause and then a third shot.

"Sounds like trouble," the bartender said. "I hope they don't bring it in here."

"Watch this for me, will you?" Longarm said, pushing his still nearly full glass across the bar.

He turned and headed out to see if there was anything that needed his help.

Chapter 5

Longarm stepped through the batwings onto a board side-walk and stopped there. It took no great powers of deduction to see what the shooting had been about. It was no robbery gone bad but appeared to be simply a private matter between two men.

One was down on the ground, his revolver lying in the dirt some feet away, while the victor stood over him with his six-gun still in hand. Both men were in the middle of the street.

Around them time seemed to have stopped. All movement had come to a halt, people standing still and staring.

The two combatants were perhaps thirty feet away from Longarm. The one on the ground struggled to a sitting position and said something to the other. Whatever it was it was too low for Longarm to overhear.

Longarm reached inside his coat for a cheroot, nipped the twist off with his teeth, and spat out the bit of tobacco. He extracted a match from another pocket, snapped it aflame with his thumbnail, and lighted his smoke. He flicked the spent match into the street and was about to return to the drink he had abandoned inside the saloon, figuring the Cheyenne police could handle this. There was no reason for him to become involved.

That intention went by the boards, though.

The winner of the shoot-out cocked his revolver and raised it. The man took deliberate aim and carefully squeezed off a shot into the chest of the man who was already down.

That gentleman cried out and was driven back down onto the ground. He probably was dead by the time his head bounced off the hard-packed dirt.

The shooter looked around before wheeling about and trotting away down the street and into an alley.

"Son of a bitch," Longarm mumbled. He looked around himself, expecting to see a Cheyenne law dog come running. After all, there had been more than enough shooting to attract the attention of one, and generally Cheyenne police were quick to respond to trouble. This time there was no one.

With a sigh of resignation, Longarm stepped down off the sidewalk and went to see if the man who was down might still somehow be alive and in need of help.

As expected, though, the only help the fellow needed would be provided by an undertaker. He was gone, his eyes open wide in the shock of his final moments, staring sightlessly now toward a clear blue sky.

Drying blood was visible high on the dead man's right shoulder. That would have been the first bullet he took, the one that knocked him down onto the street. A smaller stain was visible on his chest, directly over his heart. That would have been the murderous, deliberate killing shot when he was already down and out of the fight, his pistol lying several feet away.

He had been young, barely old enough to shave, and handsome, with curly blond hair and downy cheeks. Tonight some mother would likely be grieving for her boy and some girl weeping for a love that might have been.

The detail that made Longarm's blood run cold, though, was where that second bullet had been so precisely placed.

The young man wore a six-pointed star on his chest.

The bullet hole was in the exact center of that badge of office.

The dead boy had been an officer on the Cheyenne police force.

Chapter 6

"Of course I'd recognize the son of a bitch was I to see him again," Longarm told the Cheyenne police lieutenant, a man named Walters. He had not given a first name when he introduced himself. "He has dark hair, drooping dark brown or black mustache. 'Bout five-foot-nine or -ten. Dark eyes kinda wide set. Ears set close to his head. Red and white checked shirt and calfskin vest. Brown corduroy britches. Knee-high muleskinner boots. Remington revolver worn high on his right hip. Wasn't wearing a hat when I saw him. Neither was your man, which suggests to me that the two o' them was indoors someplace not real far from this spot when they stepped outside and drawed on one another. What else d'you want to know?"

"Ever see him before?" Walters asked.

Longarm shook his head. "Nope. Not in person nor on any wanted poster. I'm pretty sure about that."

"Look, Long, I realize you have no jurisdiction about this and no responsibility, but it bothers me that you just stood there and let someone murder one of my people in cold blood."

"Well, fuck you," Longarm snapped. "Like you said, this ain't my jurisdiction. Far as I knew it was a personal matter between two civilians, an' you folks would take care of it. When I found out the boy was one o' yours, I came and found you so's you," he stared Walters in the eye, "so's you could finally figure out that one o' your people was dead. And now you're gonna piss in my face like some part of it was my fault. You go to hell, Walters, and all your kith and kin along with you."

For a moment Walters bristled. Then the tension went out of his shoulders as he visibly got control of his emotions. "You're right. Of course you are right, Long. It is just . . . Lawrence had such promise. He was so proud of his badge. He wasn't on duty this morning. He is . . . I mean was . . . a night officer."

"So where would he have been to get into this dust-up this morning?" Longarm asked. "Find that place and it might go a long way toward finding out what happened. And who the shooter is."

"Yes. Of course. I . . ." Walters looked like he had no idea which way to turn next.

"Did the boy drink heavy or maybe was he the sort to fight over a whore?" Longarm asked.

"I . . . I don't know."

"Boss," a shout interrupted. "Hey, Lieutenant. Over here," called a police officer wearing a brass-buttoned blue coat, tan trousers, and a blue cap like a railroad conductor's but with a brass medallion on the front. "We found something."

Walters turned away and hustled over to his man. Longarm trailed along close behind out of simple curiosity.

"Jimmy was in Sol Heidrich's saloon, Lieutenant. Him and some other fellow got into a squabble over which of them would go upstairs with that redheaded new girl. The guy saw her first, but she was sweet on Jimmy and wanted to go with him. The two of them argued about it and the fellow called Jimmy out. Insulted him pretty bad, I guess. He didn't have no choice but to walk outside with this fellow."

"Who was the man?" Walters asked.

The officer shook his head. "No one in there knows, Lieutenant. Far as anybody could tell he was just some horny fellow passing through. Drover maybe or some bummer off the trains. Passenger or the like, but he wasn't a regular and nobody in there heard him give a name."

"The girl? What does she say?"

"That's Skinny Sally, Lieutenant. You remember her. Tall and, well, skinny. She says Jimmy Lawrence was a regular. Says she was sweet on him too. Let him have her for half price. But she doesn't want us to let Sol know about that or he'll give her a hiding so she won't be able to sit for a week. She never seen the other guy before."

"All right, thanks." Walters turned and almost bumped into Longarm before he saw the tall marshal standing immediately behind him. "You? What are you doing here? This is none of your business, Long."

"Of course it isn't," Longarm agreed, "but I thought you might find it helpful if you had hold of somebody that could identify the killer." He shrugged. "Reckon I was wrong about that." He politely touched the brim of his Stetson and turned away.

"Wait," Walters said. "You're right, and if we catch somebody, we will get you to identify him as Lawrence's murderer."

Longarm grunted. "I'll be in that place 'cross the street or else at the Carter House until tomorrow morning. Then I'm taking a stage out of here."

"I may want you to stay over until we catch up with this individual," Walters said.

"Sorry, but that ain't gonna happen. I got my own duties to attend to. Now, if you'll excuse me, I got half a whiskey an' a bowl o' peanuts waiting for me over there."

"Wait," Walters ordered. "I am requiring you to stay here as a witness. I can lock you up if necessary. I can get a judge to issue an order."

"Like I said before," Longarm said with a smile, "fuck you, mister." He walked away without offering any argument about it.

By then an ambulance had arrived, pulled by a handsome pair of bay cobs. The attendants were placing the young police officer onto a stretcher to carry him away somewhere. Longarm again thought of the boy's mother and how terrible her day was about to become.

Chapter 7

Longarm finished his whiskey and another one just like it, then had lunch and a stroll around town—halfway keeping an eye out for the man who had shot Officer Jimmy Lawrence—then wiled the rest of the day away with a selection of newspapers from back east.

He ended the day with another few whiskeys and a long, sound sleep. In the morning he had time for a leisurely breakfast and a shave in a friendly barbershop before heading over to the stagecoach depot. He did not hear from Lieutenant Walters or anyone else from the Cheyenne Police Department. If any local judge had issued an order for him to remain in Cheyenne, he did not know about it. Not that he'd really expected to hear anything, but it would have been good if they could have caught the shooter. Longarm hated the idea of any lawman being gunned down like Jimmy Lawrence was. As Walters had pointed out more than once yesterday, though, young Lawrence's death was not in Longarm's jurisdiction.

He reclaimed his saddle and other gear from the stage station and headed out the door.

"Wait, mister," the ticket agent called after him.

Longarm stopped and turned around. "Yes?"

"Your ticket. You don't have a ticket."

With a sigh, Longarm set his carpetbag down to free a hand. He pulled out his wallet and flipped it open to the badge there. "Deputy U.S. marshal," he said, "travelin' on official business."

Part of the line's mail contract required that federal officers have unfettered use of the coaches.

"Sorry, sir. You go right ahead."

When the time came, the coach turned out to be a rather tired and rickety army surplus mud wagon pulled by a four-up of little Spanish mules. There was no luggage shelf, and the roof was not stout enough to carry any serious weight, so luggage had to be piled at the front of the coach. Longarm tossed his things in with those of the other three passengers and climbed inside.

The seats were nothing fancier than a hard, wooden bench along each side of the coach and facing inward, toward the other bench. Entry and exit were from the rear.

A young couple sat pressed tight together on one bench. They had the look of a pair of youngsters traveling on a honeymoon, the girl probably still in her teens and the boy not much older. Whoever they were and wherever they were bound, Longarm wished them long life and happiness. He nodded and touched the brim of his Stetson when he climbed into the coach from the open doorway at the rear.

He chose a seat as far as he could get from a very obviously unwashed "gentleman" on the other bench. The man smelled. Of sweat and puke and Lord knew what else. He had the appearance of a man who was at the ass end of a weeklong drunk. Longarm hoped the fellow would not turn out to be a talkative sort.

The jehu and the station agent stopped at the back of the

coach and peered in. "Everybody settled and comfortable?" the jehu asked. He was a middle-aged fellow, slender as a whip and probably as tough as one too. He had a long, jagged scar that ran from the corner of his left eye down onto his neck. "We'll be stopping every twenty miles or so. We'll be moving fast, so hang on tight, folks."

The station agent said nothing, but he did check his watch and said something to the driver, who nodded and came forward. The coach shifted on its leather slings when the jehu climbed onto the driving box and took up his lines.

"Turn them loose, Johnny," he called out, so apparently there was a helper who was holding the mules for him. Longarm had not noticed the third fellow until the coach lurched into motion and they passed within a foot or so of a raggedy man wearing a cloth cap and coveralls.

The coach was not three miles out of town before the jehu shouted, "Whoa there. Whoa, you sons of bitches."

The young bride pretended not to have heard, while her husband scowled. Longarm suspected the young man would be having a word with the driver about his language, never mind that the girl had probably been hearing that and far worse for most of her life.

The coach came to a rocking halt, and someone pitched a pair of saddlebags in through the side, by the young couple. Longarm could see the shoulders and torso of whoever it was, but the dust curtains on that side of the wagon prevented him from seeing the face of the newcomer until he reached the back of the coach and began to climb in.

"Oh, shit," the newcomer said then.

The man who had hailed the stagecoach was the fellow who had gunned down Officer Jimmy Lawrence.

He obviously recognized Longarm as the man who had stood watching not thirty feet away when he murdered Constable Lawrence the previous day. But then the two had made eye contact before the shooter turned and ran, before Longarm knew the fight was something other than a private matter.

"This is your unlucky day," the shooter snarled. "Crawl your ass out of there, mister. You're just going to have to take the next coach north. If you're still alive and kicking, that is. Now get out. I'm on the prod and you know I mean business. You seen what I can do and I'm willing to do it again."

•

Chapter 8

With that young bride sitting so close by inside the narrow mud wagon, Longarm did not want to start a gun battle.

Besides, he would rather simply arrest the shooter.

While that asshole Walters was absolutely correct that Longarm had no jurisdiction over municipal offenses—and murder was not a federal crime—any citizen had the right to make an arrest in the absence of lawful authority.

Well, Custis Long was a citizen. So he had as much right as anyone to make a citizen's arrest.

He crawled his ass out of the coach, just like the gunman demanded.

"You being right in the neighborhood and everything," the shooter said once Longarm had his feet on the ground behind the coach, "you might just as well hand over your wallet to me. Let me see what kind of roll you're carrying."

The gunman chuckled and looked smug, mighty pleased with himself for the way this seemed to be turning out.

Longarm shuffled sideways. He wanted to make sure the coach, and the young couple inside it, was out of the line of fire if things went south from here on out.

"Funny you should mention it," he said, "I was just fixing to reach for my wallet."

"Fine. Drag it out here. I'll relieve you of the burden and you can start walking back to town. Time you get there to report anything, I'll be miles and miles away from here. Those stupid coppers won't never catch me."

"Actually," Longarm said, reaching inside his coat—with his left hand—and pulling out his wallet, "actually those stupid coppers have already caught up with you."

"What the hell are you talking about, mister?" the gunman demanded.

Longarm flipped the wallet open to display the badge pinned inside there.

"Jesus!" the gunman blurted.

"You're under arrest, shitforbrains," Longarm said. "Now, shuck that gunbelt and turn around with your hands behind your back. We'll all take a nice little ride and I'll send you back to Cheyenne directly." He was already thinking about where he could leave his prisoner for the Cheyenne authorities to come fetch the son of a bitch. In the next town with a jail, he supposed. He himself could not take the time to return the man to the Cheyenne police but . . .

The shooter did not have sense enough to leave a bad situation alone. He had to make it worse.

He went for his gun.

It was the last mistake he would ever make.

Longarm's hand flashed and his Colt belched lead, flame, and smoke.

The .45 bucked in Longarm's hand once, twice, a third time.

The gunman was driven backward with each shot. Then his legs buckled and he pitched forward, facedown in the dirt beneath his feet.

"I wish you hadn't done that," Longarm muttered.

"What the hell is going on back there?" the jehu shouted.

"Just taking care of business," Longarm said.

He checked to make sure the man was dead, then began reloading with the cartridges he carried loose in his coat pocket. "Seems you have some more freight to haul to the next town where I can get a wire off to the Cheyenne police. Now help me load this fella in, will you?"

"Just leave him there. We got a schedule to keep, you know."

"Then get down from there and give me a hand. We are *not* going to leave the man lying here."

"The hell you say. He's not going on my coach and that's that." The jehu set his jaw defiantly then turned his head and spat.

"Whatever you say, neighbor," Longarm said, pulling out his handcuffs. "Turn around."

"Now what?" the driver demanded.

Longarm shrugged. "I'm arrestin' you on a charge of obstruction of justice. You can ride in the coach and I'll drive us on to wherever I can find a jail to put you in and an undertaker for this poor son of a bitch."

"Wait. You . . . you can't do that!" the jehu wailed.

Actually the man was right. Longarm had no such authority. Probably. But he was willing to let that work itself out in front of a judge. "Turn around," Longarm repeated.

"All right. All right, dammit. We'll carry him on."

Longarm grunted. "That's better," he said. He put the handcuffs away. He did not want to pile the bloody corpse into the back of the coach with the honeymooners, so over the continuing protests of the jehu, Longarm stuffed the body onto the floor of the driving box.

"Now," Longarm said when they were done, "let's be rolling north, shall we?"

Chapter 9

It wasn't much of a town, more like a glorified crossroads, and while it almost certainly had a name, Longarm never heard what that name might be. What it did have was a telegraph key.

"Whilst I'm busy getting a wire off to the Cheyenne police," he told the driver, "you can unload the corpse and put him . . . I dunno, someplace in the shade, I s'pose. Into an ice house if they got such a thing here."

"Me?" the jehu groaned. "You shot him. You get rid of him."

Longarm shrugged. "It don't make no nevermind to me. Just leave him in the damn drivin' box if you'd rather."

"Hey!" the jehu yelped. "You can't . . ."

Longarm turned his back and walked away in search of that telegraph.

It was coming evening of the next day when he finally reached Dwyer, having traveled overnight with relays of the mules and changing coaches twice.

Dwyer, seat of McConnell County, was . . . not very

damned much. It was sun-baked and dusty, most of the boards and shingles on the buildings warping and untended. The only building of any substance was the courthouse, which was built of stone and had a copper-clad copola perched on top of a slate roof.

Longarm fetched his gear out of the coach and dropped it onto the porch in front of the general store, which apparently acted as stagecoach agent in addition to selling everything else.

A floppy-eared cur dropped its head and shyly wagged its tail at Longarm's approach. He bent down and gave the dog a scratch behind the ears before stepping inside the store. The place smelled of cinnamon and tanned leather and something else that Longarm could not quite identify. "Howdy."

The proprietor looked up and said, "Come in on the evening coach, did you?"

"I did," Longarm affirmed. "Now I'm needin' a couple things from you if I may."

"That's what I'm here for. What can I sell you?"

"What I need is information," Longarm told the man. "First off, where can I get a room for the night. Second, where can I find John Tyler?"

"You can likely do both at the same place, seeing as how we don't have a hotel here. Boys come in from working livestock, they most generally get liquored up and spend the nights at Rosie's place or else Doris's. You don't look like a man in search of a drink, so likely you'd want a room with the Tylers. John, he's the sheriff here. His wife is Nell. They're good folks. Clean. Decent. They been known to take in a boarder now and then if he looks like a decent sort himself. And you're a strong, strapping fellow. Could be you can help the Tylers around the place a little while you're there."

Longarm's left eyebrow went up at that comment. "Help them how?"

"Oh, doing the things John can't is all I mean."

"John can't what, exactly?"

The storekeeper leaned his elbows on his sales counter and stifled a yawn. "John can't do very damn much right now. That's the truth of it."

"The man is the sheriff of this county, isn't he?"

"Oh, he is that, all right."

"Then what . . . ?"

"John had a run-in with a contrary horse a couple weeks back. It fell on him, and he's been laid up in bed with a busted leg, bunch of busted ribs, and his foot broke ever since." The gentleman smiled just a little and said, "Which makes me guess you're the marshal John sent to Denver for."

"How would you know . . . ?"

"My telegraph key," the man said with a smug grin. "I get let in on lots of things."

Longarm laughed. "Right. Of course you would. Well then, can you tell me how I can get to John and Nell Tyler's place, please?"

Chapter 10

John Tyler's place was a modest two-story house on the north edge of town. It was surrounded by a whitewashed picket fence with a row of struggling rosebushes around the front porch. Longarm let himself inside the fence and waved to a man seated in a high-backed wicker chair on the forward edge of that porch, where he could see down the main street toward Dwyer's clump of businesses.

When Longarm got closer, he could see that the man had his left leg splinted and heavily wrapped. It was propped on a stool, and he had a pair of crutches lying on the porch floor beside his chair. He was a man of middle years and slight build. He had a book laid open in his lap and a shotgun lying on the porch floor beside his chair.

"You must be Tyler," Longarm said as he approached.

"*Sheriff* Tyler," the man said, emphasizing the title. For some reason he looked ready to bristle.

"I'm Long," Longarm announced.

"I don't care how tall you are, mister. Just state your business. And it better not be that you came here to act as some sort of vigilante. If I get a whiff of that sort of thing,

bum leg or not, I'll run your ass right out of my county."
Tyler sounded like he meant that too. Not that Longarm
suspected he would be capable of such a thing. The growling was all bluff. It pretty much had to be, busted up as he
was.

"You didn't get a wire about me?" he asked.

"A wire? Why should I?"

"From Marshal Billy Vail?"

"Vail? I . . . Oh, hell. You're one of Vail's deputies?"

"That's right." Longarm stepped up onto the porch and
offered his hand. "Custis Long," he said, "but most call me
Longarm."

Tyler looked embarrassed. "I apologize for that, Longarm. It's just . . . I guess I don't adjust so easy to being laid
up. It drives me crazy that I can't get around. The doc says
it will be weeks before I can walk again, and then it will
be with this accursed splint still on my leg. Won't be able
to ride except for in a damned buggy for maybe a couple
months, and this is a big county that I'm responsible for.
That's why I asked Marshal Vail for help." He motioned
Longarm toward a ladder-back rocker sitting nearby on the
porch.

"Billy said you got a war brewing between sheepmen
and goatherds?" Longarm said, setting his things down and
taking a seat on the rocking chair.

Tyler nodded. "Exactly. There is some good grazing up
here. Very good grass in some places, scrub in others, and
one stream running through the valley those fellows are
fixing to fight over. What we have are two factions. The
sheepmen are Basques out of some place over there in
Europe. Spain, I think, but God knows what that language
is that they speak. It sure isn't Spanish. Then there's the
goatherds. They're Mexican. Neither bunch is all that good
with speaking English. Both of them want that valley for

their animals. I've heard rumors that they intend to arm themselves, maybe even bring in professional gunslingers, and fight it out. The winner gets the grass and the loser gets laid out underneath it."

"And here you sit on your front porch," Longarm said.

"Exactly."

Longarm grunted. "Then between you knowing your county and me being able to get around in it, maybe the two of us can head this off."

"That's what I'm hoping, Deputy."

"Which reminds me," Longarm said. "Why is it that your own deputies can't handle this for you? Surely they aren't choosing up sides in this deal too."

"I don't have deputies. This is a poor county. We can't afford to pay for even one deputy. And the town doesn't have a marshal either. Unfortunately, I'm all the law enforcement there is in McConnell County."

"Makes it hard with you bein' laid up an' all," Longarm observed.

"Exactly."

"While we're on the subject," Longarm said, "I'll have jurisdiction here because of you asking for our help. That's the law. But just to keep things on the up-and-up, it might be a good idea for you to swear me in as a county deputy acting under your authority too." He grinned. "Without pay, of course."

"I can do that," Tyler said, nodding. "Tomorrow morning mayhap you can go down to the courthouse with me and we can make it official. I'll have you sworn in by our county clerk."

"That settles that," Longarm said. "Now there's just one thing more."

"And that would be . . . ?"

"The fella down to the general store said you and

your missus sometimes takes in boarders. Would it be possible . . ."

Before Longarm could finish, Tyler raised up a bit in his chair and shouted, "Nell! Come out here, old woman. We got a houseguest for you to see to."

Chapter 11

John Tyler's "old woman" looked like she was barely out of her teens and maybe not that old. She was at most half her husband's age. She was not very pretty, a little too much on the scrawny side for beauty, but she had a grand smile and her welcome was very obviously genuine.

"Deputy Long, you said? Well, welcome to our home, Mr. Long." She held her hand out to shake like a man, first wiping it clean on the apron that covered a plain house-dress. Her hand, Longarm noticed when he took it, was hard and calloused. He suspected that this was a woman who took her housekeeping seriously.

"The marshal will be staying with us for a while, dear," Tyler informed her.

She beamed. "How nice. John is weary of having only me to talk with. It is bad enough during the day, but at least in daylight he can sit out here and watch down the street. At night he drives me crazy." She laughed. "All the more so because I beat him at cribbage eight times out of ten."

"You exaggerate," Tyler chimed in.

"Seven and a half then," Nell said.

Longarm chuckled. "Then you'll both be glad to hear that I am a perfectly awful cribbage player."

"Have you eaten yet, Mr. Long?"

He shook his head. "No, I just got in a few minutes ago."

Nell smiled. "Then your timing is perfect. We will be sitting down to the table as soon as my potatoes are done."

"I don't want to put you out, Miz Tyler. You weren't expectin' me."

She waved her hand dismissively. "You'll not put us out. We always have enough for an extra plate or two."

"Then I reckon will join you and thanks."

"Bring your things inside, Marshal. I will show you to your room and start putting things on the table. When you are settled in, you can come downstairs and keep John company until I call you two to supper."

"You're mighty kind, ma'am," Longarm said, removing his Stetson as he followed Nell inside their very tidy home.

Nell showed him to a small bedroom upstairs at the back of the house. It smelled of fresh air and sunshine.

"Please excuse the mess downstairs, Mr. Long. It isn't easy for John to manage stairs with his crutches so he has been sleeping on the sofa. If you need anything during the night, you can wake me. I sleep in that bedroom there," she said, pointing toward a door at the front of the house. "I'm a light sleeper, and I am up several times during the night to check on John, so do tap on my door if you need anything."

"You're mighty kind, ma'am," he said again.

"All right then. I'll go back to my kitchen. I'll call you two when supper is ready."

Nell gathered up her skirts and scampered down the narrow and rather steep staircase. It was no wonder Tyler could not negotiate the stairs on his crutches.

Longarm turned back into his bedroom to unpack the few things he'd brought and prepare for the evening.

Chapter 12

Nell Tyler's dinner was every bit as good as anything he could have found in the finest hotels in Denver. Maybe better. Longarm laid his fork aside and put his napkin on the table beside his plate. "That was fine, ma'am. John, you got yourself a good'un here."

Both Tylers seemed pleased by the compliments.

"Cribbage, Longarm?" Tyler asked.

"If you don't mind, John, I'd like to wander around in the town a little. See what I run into. Eavesdrop on the bar talk. I'm sure you understand."

Tyler nodded. "Indeed, I do." He turned his head and said, "Dear, would you excuse us for a few minutes, please."

"Oh, piffle. I know what your man talk will be about. You intend to tell Custis that the Basque sheepherders drink and . . . whatever . . . at Rosie's but the Mexican goatherds go to Doris's."

"I think I don't want to know how you know that," her husband said.

Longarm had to hide a smile that kept tugging at the corners of his lips. It seemed that Nell Tyler was quite a handful.

Tyler gave Longarm a half-apologetic, half-embarrassed shrug and said, "That is exactly what I intended to tell you."

Longarm let the laugh out and rose from the table. "Then if you will excuse me, I'll leave the two of you to get into your fight without me to interfere."

John Tyler remained seated. "I would go with you, Longarm, but . . ."

"Could be better this way anyhow," Longarm said. "For the first little while there won't nobody know who I am or what I'm doin' here. Once they do know, they'll like to clam up. As just a passing stranger, I might could hear something interesting."

"Our door is never locked so let yourself in whenever you want," Nell told him.

"Thank you, ma'am, and thank you for that fine supper too." Longarm plucked his Stetson off the hat rack beside the door and let himself out into the evening air, cool almost to the point of being chilly.

He walked the short distance to town and stopped for a moment in front of the handsome courthouse. He would be seeing more of that come tomorrow, but for now he was content just to get the feel of the town.

There were three saloons, Rosie's, Doris's, and one no-name little outfit where, judging from the lack of traffic in and out of its doors, a man could get nothing more than a drink and perhaps a game of billiards.

The two that also served as whorehouses for the solitary herdsmen were situated on opposite corners a block and a half from the courthouse. Both were brightly lighted and very active, with men streaming in and out frequently. The sounds of piano music came from one of them, but from a distance Longarm could not tell from which.

Since he was at least a little bit familiar with Mexicans,

to the point anyway of having met a good many, he headed for Doris's place first.

When Longarm arrived, the saloon was busy; the noise made by a trio of minstrels and the singing that went with their music practically hit him a physical blow when he walked in the door. He had no idea what they were singing about or what sort of song it might have been, as it was sung entirely in Spanish. As an Anglo adrift in a sea of Mexicans, he felt a little out of place.

A long bar ran down the wall on the left. Tables—well-attended ones—filled much of the floor, while at the back he could see a rather limp and wilted-looking whore passing by one table after another, offering herself to one and all. A good many of the patrons were eating something out of large wooden bowls, while virtually everyone had a beer or a shot on the table. Or both.

"Help you?" the bartender asked when Longarm presented himself at the bar.

"Beer, please."

"Ten cents."

Longarm laid his money down while the bartender drew a beer, leaving much too much head on it. The man took Longarm's dime without a word and stepped a few paces down the bar, where he got into an animated conversation in Spanish.

Longarm took a swallow of the crisply refreshing beer but left most of it on the bar untouched. He could spend the next three nights standing there and not learn a thing, as he could grasp the meaning of not one word in twenty.

Back on the street, he wondered if there was any point in going over to Rosie's, or if the talk there would be as unintelligible as it had been in Doris's.

There was only one way to find out.

The result was just as bad as at Doris's, with the exception that in Rosie's place there were two Anglos in search of the whores. Those ladies of the night were busy at this post-dinner hour. A fellow had to wait for one of them to become available.

Longarm stayed long enough to drink a beer. And to decide there was less than no point in trying to eavesdrop on the Basques. Their language—he asked—was called Euskara, and it was like nothing else he'd ever heard.

At least the bartender was a little more pleasant than the one across the street. And the whores were a hell of a lot better looking.

Longarm finished the last of his beer—the suds had not been nearly as deep on the beer he was served in Rosie's— and left a nickel tip for the barman, then left.

He still wanted to find a little better evening entertainment than playing cribbage with John and Nell Tyler, so he walked down the street to the no-name saloon, where he found peace and quiet save for the clicking of billiard balls.

Better than the quiet, he also found a good label of rye whiskey in the no-name place.

And the barman was a woman. Not a bad-looking woman, except for the fact that she looked big enough and tough enough to knock heads if things became rowdy on a Saturday night.

"You look like a man who's found what he was looking for," she said when he leaned on her bar.

"I am," he told her, pointing to the row of bottles on the back wall. "See that one, third from the left. I'd like a glass o' that, if you please."

"Fifteen cents," she said. "You want a beer to go with that?"

Longarm shook his head. "No, I wouldn't want anything to wash that fine flavor off my tongue."

The lady nodded her approval and brought the bottle and a small tumbler. "My name is Helen," she said when she had set the glass down and poured a generous measure of rye.

"I'm Custis."

"You're the marshal up here from Denver, aren't you?"

He gave her a quizzical look. Helen laughed and said, "Samuel Johnson over at the mercantile has a big mouth. He came in here after he closed up for the night. He said the federal man from Denver got in this afternoon, and since you're the only stranger I've seen in town lately, well, you pretty much have to be him."

"I plead guilty," Longarm told her. "Say this really is good stuff." The rye lay smooth and warm on his tongue before he swallowed it.

"If there is anything I can do to help you while you're here," Helen said, "just let me know." She smiled. "I have a vested interest in this community. I want it to be safe and prosperous."

"You don't seem to do much business with the, um, live-stock raisers," he observed.

"Not directly, I don't, but if the town prospers, then so do the men who are my customers. Like I said. A vested interest."

"Fair enough." He swallowed the rest of his rye.

"Another?"

He nodded, and Helen poured, this time an even more generous amount.

Longarm decided he had found the place where he would be spending his leisure time while he was in Dwyer.

Chapter 13

"Did you learn anything last night?" John Tyler asked as Longarm seated himself at the breakfast table.

"Sure did," Longarm responded. "Learned I won't be doing any eavesdropping around either bunch o' those fellas. I couldn't understand a word they was sayin'." He glanced up to see if Nell was nearby. She was not, so he continued, "I also found a place that serves real good whiskey."

"That would be Helen Birch's place," Tyler said.

"That's right. She said her name is Helen. She owns it?"

Tyler nodded. "She and her husband came here about, oh, five years ago. He opened the saloon while she tended to the home. Then Cory . . . that was her husband's name, Cory . . . he let things get a little too rowdy one night and got himself stabbed for his troubles. The man lingered for nearly a month before he finally died. They say the dying was a real blessing as he'd been stabbed in the stomach. Gangrene got all through his body." Tyler shrugged. "Everybody thought Helen would sell out or just close up after Cory was gone, but she opened the place back up and has kept it going ever since. She runs a good place. Won't allow any ladies of the night, though, and won't tolerate any troubles in her place."

"She looks big enough to enforce that," Longarm said.

"Oh, she is. She keeps a bung starter under the counter, and she isn't afraid to bust a man's head open with it if he steps out of line."

Longarm smiled. "I'll try an' keep that in mind."

Nell came out of the kitchen bearing a tray that was piled high with flapjacks and pork chops and fried potatoes.

"It is a wonderful thing that you are here, Longarm," John Tyler said. "When we're alone, all I get for breakfast is oatmeal and coffee."

Nell set the tray down and gave her husband a swat on the back of his head, then went back into her kitchen for the coffeepot to offer John a refill and in Longarm's case his first cup of the day.

After breakfast, Longarm helped Tyler out onto the porch, where the man settled into his chair with a sigh. "I hate being laid up this way," he said, "but letting that damned bronc bust me up like this is my own fault. I should've bailed off him when I felt him slip, but I thought I could ride the bastard down." He grimaced. "I was wrong."

"You might find this hard to believe," Longarm said, pulling a cheroot from his pocket and lighting it, "but I was wrong about something once my own self."

"Really?" Tyler said with mock surprise. "I never would've guessed it. If you don't mind me changing the subject, what do you intend to do now?"

"If you'll tell me where I can rent a horse," Longarm said, puffing contentedly on his cigar and blowing a few smoke rings, "reckon I will ride out and talk to whoever is in charge of those two groups of herders."

"We have a livery the second block west of the court-house, which reminds me. I need to take you down there to swear you in as a McConnell County special deputy. Mind if I ask you to hitch our mare up to the buggy so I can get down there? I suppose I could make it that far on crutches, but I'd rather not try."

"That's no bother at all," Longarm said. "We can take care of that, then I'll rent me a horse after. You got a barn out back?"

"We do."

"Big enough to handle a visiting animal?" Longarm asked.

"Big enough," Tyler said, "and plenty of grass hay and mixed feed grain too."

"Then if you don't mind, I'll tell your liveryman that I'll keep the animal for as long as I need him. Just in case I need to go someplace in a hurry, I won't have to waste time walking over to the livery."

"I understand."

"Thinking of renting," Longarm said, "we haven't spoke yet about how much I need t' pay for my room an' board."

Tyler waved the question away with a sweep of his hand. "You're here to help me and you're staying in my house. Nell and I wouldn't think of charging you rent."

"Thanks." Longarm resolved to do something to help defray the cost of his keep while he was staying with the Tylers. Groceries, perhaps, or something else Nell would appreciate. He stood. "Now if you'll excuse me, I'll go find that buggy o' yours an' bring it around front when I have it hitched an' ready."

Chapter 14

Longarm left Tyler's sleek little chestnut mare tied to an iron post shaped to look like a jockey, although one whose paint was chipped and peeling. He helped Tyler out of the buggy and up the courthouse steps.

"Over this way," Tyler said, pointing toward a door that read COUNTY CLERK on the frosted glass panel. "My office is in the basement. One good-sized room and two small cells. Around back there's an entrance from the outside. I'll give you a key so you can come and go as you please."

Longarm opened the door to the clerk's office and stood aside while Tyler made his way inside on the crutches.

There were three men in the office, laboring over ledgers and piles of paper. Longarm had no idea what could possibly require the efforts of three clerical workers in a county as sparsely populated as McConnell . . . but then it sometimes seemed to him that the first order of business for any government agency was to expand itself. At the expense of its taxpayers. Apparently that rule was no different here than in Denver.

"Benjamin, this is the gentleman I told you would be coming," Tyler said.

The oldest of the three workers, a slender man with thinning, gray hair, looked up from his ledgers and smiled. He rose and came to the counter, where he extended his hand. "Benjamin Laffler," he said.

"Custis Long," Longarm said in return, taking the man's hand to shake.

"What can I do for you gents?" Laffler asked.

"I want to swear Custis in as a McConnell deputy, Ben. We need for you to witness the oath and record it."

"Can we afford . . . ?"

"He will serve without pay," Tyler cut in.

Laffler said, "In that case, Long, welcome to our county. Wait just a moment while I fetch a Bible and we can do this."

Three minutes later, having affirmed his fealty, Longarm was a duly sworn officer of McConnell County, Wyoming Territory.

"There are some badges in my desk downstairs," Tyler told him, "or you can just continue to use your own. Benjamin, do you have any extra keys to the sheriff's office?"

"I do. I'll get one for you." He turned away and went to the back of the room, to a file cabinet, where he began rummaging inside a lower drawer. A minute later he was back with a key for the new deputy.

"Do you want to go down to your office?" Longarm asked when they were again in the hallway outside the clerk's office.

Tyler shook his head. "That would be too much, I think. I'd have to go down the steps outside then all the way around the building and down those steps too. It's just . . . Not until I get off these damned crutches, if you don't mind."

"Makes no nevermind t' me, John, and in that case let's get you home. I'll beg one more cup o' Nell's good coffee and then go see what I can do toward having a saddle horse."

"Fine," Tyler said. When he was again settled onto the seat of the buggy, he grumbled, "These crutches might not be so bad except the damn things cut into my armpits no matter how Nell tries to pad them. Lordy, I will be glad when I can get rid of them."

He drove to his house and as close as he could get to the front gate, then said, "If you don't mind taking it from here, this is the shortest way into the house."

"Don't mind at all," Longarm said.

Longarm secured the mare to a hitching weight, then helped Tyler down from the buggy and back to his chair on the front porch. He tapped on the door and told Nell they were back, then returned to the buggy and drove it around to the little barn in back of the house.

He stripped the harness from the mare and hung it, secured the horse in her stall, and parked the buggy under an overhang at the side of the barn. By the time he returned to the front of the house, there was a cup of steaming hot coffee waiting for him.

"Herself wants to know if you will be back for lunch," Tyler said, inclining his head toward the house—as if there were any question just who he meant by "herself."

"No, I expect not," Longarm said, taking a swallow that quickly turned into a careful sip of the very hot coffee. "I'll get me a horse an' then see how things go from there. Any idea where I can find these sheepmen an' goatherds?"

"Easy enough. Just ride up the valley. You'll see their camps and their flocks scattered every damn place you look. There isn't any one person in charge of either bunch, though. They are all independent as hell. And twice as ornery."

"All right then." Longarm sat until he finished the coffee, then got up and excused himself. "I'd set an' visit awhile, but what I come here to do is serious stuff. Reckon I shouldn't keep it waiting for my laziness."

"We'll expect you back when we see the whites of your eyes," Tyler said, "whenever that might be."

"Fair enough." Longarm shook the man's hand and headed for Dwyer's livery.

Chapter 15

"I'm looking for a fella name of Anthony," Longarm said to the young man who was busy braiding horsehair.

The young fellow looked up from his work. "That would be me," he said.

Longarm was surprised. Hostlers were generally older men who had decided to retire from the rugged work of a cowhand or wrangler but could not stand to completely give up the game. Anthony DeCaro was anything but that stereotype. He looked like a city boy—with the emphasis on "boy"—yet John Tyler had vouched for DeCaro's knowledge and abilities.

"I'm the . . ."

"I know who you are," DeCaro said with a grin. "The whole town does. Probably the whole county by now."

Longarm could only shake his head in wonder. The town of Dwyer seemed to have faster communications than Denver's telephone system could have offered. "I need . . ."

"I know what you need," DeCaro said. "You'll be wanting a saddle horse to use while you're up here."

"That's right," Longarm said. "The sheriff said you know

your horses and you're honest. He suggested I get you to pick something out for me."

"I'll be happy to do that," the young livery stable owner said. "First though I have a question for you. Are you looking for a horse that's fast or one that's steady? That is, do you expect to be chasing after someone or will you be riding off the road and want a horse you can count on to not stumble?"

"Steady," Longarm told him. "If I do my job right, I won't have t' be running no horse races across bad country."

"Then I have a good one for you. He won't win any races if you do get into any, but you can count on him to take you wherever you want to go without getting busted up like John was."

"Then drag him out here, son, and let me take a look at him."

The horse DeCaro brought in from a corral behind the barn was a light-bodied dun, perhaps fourteen hands tall or a finger less, with brown points and a small muzzle. The feet were so small and delicate Longarm wondered how the little horse would manage over rough ground.

"Don't be put off by his looks," DeCaro said. "His blood is some foreign breed . . . I'm not sure exactly what . . . but he's tough as whang leather and twice as steady. Smart too. I saw him get his foot in a wrap of loose wire once. Most horses would panic and try to pull away. Pull their feet clean off if they tried that. This little guy stood there like a rock, like he had as much sense as a mule. He waited for someone to come and unwrap that wire from around him. Right then and there I decided to buy him, and I'm still glad that I did. If it tells you anything, he's the horse I ride myself when I go up in the hills hunting."

"Your recommendation is good enough for me," Longarm said, going around the horse and checking his feet one by one. The little dun gave his feet without a fuss and stood steady until Longarm was done with each.

"Turn around," DeCaro said.

"All right, but why?" Longarm asked as he turned to face away.

"I'm not trying to admire your butt, marshal. I'm trying to decide what size saddle will you need."

"Oh, I won't be needing a saddle from you. I brought my own. Left it at John's place, though, to avoid havin' to lug it over here. But I will be wanting the use of your bit and bridle. Whatever the horse is used to."

"He has a soft mouth. A snaffle is all I use on him, though some customers demand a curb bit. No spades though. I won't permit a spade bit on any of my animals."

"A snaffle is fine," Longarm said. He normally used the army's tack on borrowed remount horses. The army used fairly harsh curb bits on all their horses. But then nearly all of their horses were rough and needed the extra control that the curb gave.

"Let me get one." DeCaro stepped into the tack room of his barn and emerged moments later carrying a very handsome bridle and bit made of a deep red cordovan leather and decorated with German silver brightwork.

"You give your customers fine tack to use," Longarm observed.

DeCaro smiled. "It's my own," he said. "He's used to it."

"Thanks for trusting me with it."

The hostler shrugged. "John sent you. If he trusts you, so do I."

"I'll give you a voucher redeemable from the federal government for the use of him. He'll be stabled behind the sheriff's place. I'm sure you know it."

DeCaro nodded. "That's fine. I'll bring over some feed

for him. That will be on my bill too. That way he won't be eating up what John has there."

"Fair enough," Longarm said.

DeCaro slipped the bridle over the dun's head and let him mouth the bit for a moment before he turned the reins over to Longarm. "I named him George, but of course he doesn't come to it no more than any other horse would. One thing he does well is ground rein. I wouldn't do that with any other animal I got here, but you can trust George on a ground rein.

"That's good to know," Longarm said. He arranged the reins, then sprang onto the little horse's back. Touching the brim of his Stetson toward DeCaro by way of a salute, he nudged the dun in the side. As soon as they were out of the barn, he touched the horse again and lifted it into an easy trot back to the Tyler house to pick up his gear.

It was still fairly early in the day, plenty early enough to begin speaking with whatever herdsmen he could find in the valley.

Chapter 16

A wisp of pale smoke was visible above a fold in the land about halfway up the west side of the valley. Longarm reined the dun away from the stream and nudged it into a trot. The horse crested the top of the rise, and Longarm could see a moving sea of woolly sheep—albeit a small sea— white against the brown and green of the rocky hillside.

A wagon, covered with canvas but with tall, wooden sides, sat on the uphill side of the sheep. A clutch of men squatted around a fire beside the wagon, while farther up-hill there were three horses grazing. Two of the horses were heavy-bodied animals with broad butts and cropped tails. The other looked like an ordinary cow pony.

The sheep were under the watchful eyes of perhaps a dozen dogs that lay in the grass nearby, ready to fend off predators. Longarm saw a small bunch of ewes try to escape the flock. Instantly there was a dog racing to head them off and turn them back to the group. One of the men beside the fire stood and gave a series of whistles that seemed to mean something to the dog, which instantly charged the lead ewe, nipping and barking until the shepherd's commands were obeyed. Once the sheep were back in the flock, the dog lay down while the man resumed his seat by the fire.

Longarm kneed the dun ahead. When he was within a hundred yards of the fire, the men spotted him. Moving almost as one, they stood and picked up rifles that he had not noticed from a distance.

Well, Tyler's wire to Billy Vail had said there could be a range war brewing up here. These boys looked like they were ready to start the fight right here and now.

Longarm continued his approach at a slow walk, and as he neared the Basques, he held a hand up palm outward to show he posed no danger.

"Anybody here speak English?" he called.

"I do," came an answer in a voice that sounded more Texas than Spain.

The speaker stepped forward. He was a lanky fellow with a mustache that drooped a good couple inches south of his chin. He wore a black hat with a Montana peak and a flat brim and sported a pair of revolvers, one hung at his right side and the other rigged for a cross-draw much like Longarm's outfit. Even from a distance Longarm got the impression that this fellow could be salty.

"Stop right there," he said in a husky voice once Longarm was within a dozen yards of the fire. "State your business."

"United States deputy marshal," Longarm said, "so stand your men down or get ready to have hell come calling."

The Texan turned and said something to the others, who quickly dropped the muzzles of their rifles. Several resumed squatting beside the fire and went back to a meal that Longarm seemed to have interrupted. To Longarm the English-speaking man said, "Come ahead, Marshal. We heard there was a federal man coming. Didn't know you was already here."

Longarm approached the group but stopped the dun and dismounted a little way downwind so he would not kick up dust that could get into the pots of food dangling over the fire.

He dropped the reins, hoping DeCaro was right and the dun would stand to the rein without wandering off to graze, then he approached the Texan and stuck his hand out to shake. "Custis Long," he said, "out of Marshal William Vail's Denver office."

The gent shook and said, "Eli Cruikshank." He added a small, slightly twisted grin that twitched the dangling ends of his mustache, and said, "Out of my daddy's balls in Beeville, Texas."

"Pleased t' meet you, Eli. What's your deal in this? I hope you ain't here t' be part o' the war I heard was coming to a boil up this way."

"No, not really. The bossman hired me 'cause I got a way with languages. Pick them up pretty easy. Good thing too because none of these boys can speak much in the way of English. I'm here to interpret more than anything else."

"But if there was to come a shooting war?" Longarm asked.

Cruikshank's answer was a shrug. Which told quite enough. He was there to ride for the brand, so if things came to a fight, he would be in the thick of it. Looked like he could handle himself too. Longarm hoped he would not have to face the Texas boy across the barrels of their pistols . . . all the more so because Cruikshank seemed a likeable fellow and Longarm would hate to have to kill him.

"Come set," Cruikshank said. "We're having a bite of dinner. You're welcome to share."

"Thankee kindly." Longarm fetched a tin plate and a cup out of a bucket close to the fire and helped himself to coffee, beans, and a chunk of some sort of meat. The Basques shifted somewhat away from him, as if he were contaminated with some disease that they did not care to catch.

"This ain't bad," he said after he got into the meat. "What is it?"

"Mountain lion," Cruikshank said. "Tasty stuff, isn't it? The boys favor it and kill one whenever they can to keep it from taking any of the sheep. It's kind of a bonus that they cook up so good."

Longarm nodded. "I heard they were good eating. Now I know for my own self."

"What brings you here, Marshal?" Cruikshank asked, after giving Longarm the courtesy of letting him finish his dinner before they got down to business.

"Making rounds," Longarm said. "Showing the flag, you might say. Letting everyone know that there *will* be law an' order around here."

Cruikshank snorted. "Tell that to the greasers. They're the ones making threats."

"Oh, I will tell it to them, but what's the deal with you and your Basques?"

"They're good fellows. Decent. Hard workers. Not afraid to stand up to wolves or mountain lions carrying nothing but staves or shepherd's crooks. I like them."

"Funny-looking staves," Longarm said, pointedly looking at one of the Winchesters propped against a rock close to the fire.

Cruikshank shrugged and went on, "They work for Mr. Brent Wisner up in Billings, same as I do. He owns the sheep. They work for wages and a share of the increase. Used to be the outfit was scattered all over this valley, but since the Mex'cans came here and started making threats, they stay pretty much bunched up like this for safety. O' course after dinner they'll split the flock into smaller groups and graze out; then toward dark they'll gather 'em up again. Used to be we could trust the dogs to keep watch overnight. Nowadays we post sentinels. You should ought to know that. If you come up on us at night, make sure you sing out who you are before you get close to the sheep. We, uh, we wouldn't want to make no mistakes." He grinned again. "Not by accident anyhow."

"I'll keep that in mind," Longarm said, reaching for the coffeepot for a refill. "One thing you might wanta know is that I don't intimidate real easy." He looked square into Cruikshank's eyes. "We wouldn't wanta have any o' those accidents, you an' me."

Cruikshank's answer was a grin. The Texan did not look any more intimidated than Longarm was.

It is good to know the opposition, Longarm thought. But it is even better if there is no opposition. After all, Billy had sent him up here to head off a war, not to fight one.

"Can I pour you another cup?" he asked.

"I'd like that," Cruikshank said, reaching for his cup. "Thanks."

Chapter 17

Longarm had his lunch with the Basques—and came to his unspoken understanding with Eli Cruikshank—so he then excused himself and stepped back onto the little dun named George.

"Thank you, Eli." He touched the brim of his Stetson and said, "Keep 'em out of trouble, hear?" In a soft voice he added, "An' yourself too."

"Oh, I never cause trouble, Marshal," Cruikshank grinned, "but I'm generally up for any that comes my way."

Longarm grunted and gently touched the dun's side with his heel. The horse headed downhill to the creek.

The water there flowed swift and cold, but nowhere did it appear to be deep.

Longarm could not help but notice as he splashed across that the stream was lousy with trout. They lay facing upstream, lazily finning and waiting for something edible to come floating by. It was just a damned shame that he had not come here to fish. An even worse shame that he had not thought to pass himself off as a fisherman. He might have picked up all sorts of information if neither the Basques nor the Mexicans knew who and what he was.

It was too late for that, however. Dammit!

Unlike with the Basques and their sheep, the flocks of goats and their Mexican herders were not conveniently bunched up where he could get a look at them—and they at him—all at one time.

Whereas the sheep had been herded together into one huge flock, the goats were scattered all to hell and gone in small groups of twenty or thirty animals or so. Like the sheep, the goats were being controlled more by dogs than by men, an efficient and inexpensive method.

Longarm spent the afternoon riding from one small group to another. Several key differences from the shepherds struck him along the way, apart from the way every lone goatherd looked at him with nervous suspicion when he approached.

The first was that there seemed to be no spokesman for the Mexican goatherds. At least no English-speaking spokesman that Longarm could find. The goatherds spoke Spanish, and that was that. Trying to question them only frustrated both the herder and himself.

The other major difference that was visible to Longarm's inquiring eye was that while the Mexicans were also armed, the Basques had been carrying modern Winchester or Marlin repeating lever-action rifles, but the Mexicans were armed with an assortment of old shotguns and Springfield trapdoor rifles, probably cast-off—and very likely worn out— army surplus.

If it came to a war, Longarm thought, the Basques would have a huge advantage. Not only were they much better armed, they had Eli Cruikshank on their side. Longarm suspected that Cruikshank was about as close to being a professional as you could come.

If it came to a war, he thought, it was apt to be a slaughter of the Mexicans.

He hoped it would not come to that.

It was his job to make damned sure that it did not.

Chapter 18

It was well past dark when Longarm got back to Dwyer. Lights showed in the windows of virtually all the houses in town but practically none of the storefronts. It seemed that Dwyer was a town that closed up early. The saloons were open but nothing else that he could see. That included the one café in town, a place called, coincidentally, enough, Café. At least that was what the sign over the door said. At the moment it was as dark and empty as everything else around it.

Longarm did not know exactly what time it was, but he was sure it was much too late to expect Nell Tyler to prepare a meal for him. Beer and peanuts would just have to do, he figured. He took the dun to John Tyler's barn, unsaddled it and gave it a generous measure of grain, then briefly curried and brushed it before walking over to Helen Birch's saloon.

But then he had had worse more than once in the past. There were times when beer and peanuts would have been a blessing.

"My goodness, Marshal. You look like shit," Helen said by way of greeting.

"Thank you so much. Where is everybody?"

"At home in bed like honest folks should be at this time of night," she said. Then the woman laughed and added, "Which tells you something about you and me, doesn't it? But the fact is, I was just about to close up for the night."

"All right. Sorry," he said, turning back toward the door.

"No." She stopped him. "Don't go. What can I get you?"

Longarm leaned on the bar and said, "A feather bed an' about ten hours o' sleep oughta do it. But I'll settle for a quick shot an' then leave you t' get on home."

"Have you had any supper?" she asked.

He shook his head and yawned. "No, but that's all right. Shove that bowl o' peanuts over here, would you? I'll take a handful o' them. I can set on one o' those benches over by the courthouse an' shell the little sons o' bitches."

Helen chuckled. "I think I can do better than that. I haven't had supper yet myself, so why don't you join me?"

"Lady, that's the best offer I've had all day. Thanks."

"It will be nice to have company for a change." She smiled. "I deal with people all day every day, but I never have any company, if you see what I mean."

"Sure. It's the difference between workin' and visitin'. I get the same thing, I expect."

"So you will do it?" she asked.

"I'd be pleased to." He yawned again.

Helen lived in rooms behind her saloon. She turned the OPEN sign in the window over so that it read CLOSED instead and pulled the roller blind down before she bolted the door and extinguished all but one of the lamps burning along the walls. "This way," she said, indicating a door behind the bar.

Helen went in first; she struck a match and lighted a

lamp, then turned the wick up and lighted two more before she was satisfied. "I cook simple rather than fancy," she warned.

"Simple is fine by me," Longarm said.

"It seems I've caught you at a good time for my brand of cooking." She laughed. "You're too tired to know if it's good or bad. Truth is, I'm not much of a cook. But I'll thank you to keep from saying so. To my face anyway."

"Like you said, I'm too damn weary t' know the difference tonight."

"Sit over there, Custis. I'll stir up the coals and get things moving."

"Is there anything I can do?" he asked.

"There is. You can stay out of the way. Would you like a shot or a beer to hold you off?"

"No, I'm fine. Really." He sat where Helen indicated and watched while first she built up the fire inside a cast iron stove no larger than a sheepherder-style camp stove, then poured water and put it on to heat for coffee. Once that was done, she dropped a large nugget of lard into a skillet and sliced in a generous mess of spuds. She sliced slabs of bacon into the same skillet and set it onto the fire.

"Now we wait," she said, joining Longarm at the table. "Tell me about your day," she offered.

He found himself doing exactly that. He told himself he hoped to get a local perspective on the situation in McConnell County. The truth was that Helen Birch was a good listener, and Custis Long was half-asleep and in a mood to talk with the handsome woman.

He rattled on right through the process of cooking—she was right; cooking was not one of her talents—and on through the meal. By the time the simple meal was finished, he had pretty much exhausted the subject of his rather frustrating day.

"It's the Mexicans I can't get a handle on," he told her. "The Basques at least have one English-speaking fella I can talk to."

"That would be Eli," she said.

"You know him?"

"Of course I know him. Maybe you haven't noticed, but Dwyer is a small town. I know everybody. Besides, Eli doesn't only visit the girls at Rosie's. Sometimes he likes to come here for a quiet drink."

"Right. Anyway, the Mexicans I can't talk to. Do you know anything about them making threats to the Basques?"

"I've heard the rumor," Helen said. "I don't know how true it is."

"The Basques believe it. I suppose in a manner of speaking that makes it true enough."

"True enough to cause trouble," Helen agreed. She yawned. "Excuse me."

Longarm very quickly followed suit with a yawn of his own. "Damn things are contagious, aren't they?"

"Yes, and I've often wondered why the sight of one person yawning makes everybody around them yawn too. Look, can I be straightforward with you, Custis?"

"Of course. Please do."

"I run a business here, a business where men drink, sometimes get drunk. I have to hold myself a little apart in a small town like this. Do you understand?"

"Yes, I think so," he said.

"It would cause no end of trouble if I was to fuck around, you will excuse the expression."

He grinned. "I've heard it before."

"Yes, well, it's true. I don't dare have affairs. The town's wives would find out about it, and their husbands would not be stepping inside my door again. It would ruin me. But I am not an old woman and I'm horny. More than a cucumber can take care of. Would you very much mind giving this horny woman a roll in the hay?"

"Has anybody ever accused you o' being too subtle?" Longarm asked.

Helen laughed. "No. Never."

"Good, because it wouldn't have been true." He pushed back from the table and stood.

"Are you leaving? Have I scared you away?" she asked.

"No, woman, I'm headin' for the bedroom. If you'll show me the way to it, that is."

Chapter 19

Helen Birch was not a fancy woman. Her bedroom was a small, mostly bare chamber without windows or adornments. It contained a dark walnut wardrobe, a washstand that held a basin and pitcher, and an iron bedstead with a thin mattress and a pair of blankets on it. Underneath the bed was a plain crockery thunder mug and a pair of high-topped shoes that she likely wore for dress-up occasions. The only thing on the rough plank walls was one lamp, which Helen lighted and turned up high.

"Sit down," she said.

There was only one place to sit, so he perched on the side of the bed. The springs creaked, and for a moment he wondered if his weight would be too much for them, but they held with no problem.

Helen knelt at Longarm's feet and, smiling, pulled his boots off. She set them under the bed, next to her spare shoes. Then the woman stood and began disrobing.

She was a big woman, with a thick waist and heavy thighs and surprisingly small ankles and delicate feet. She had a heavy thatch of pubic hair that was beginning to turn

gray—he suspected she put some sort of color on her hair
to keep the gray from showing there—and large, pendulous
breasts.

Her dark red areolae were as large as saucers, covering
most of her tits, with nipples like thumbs. Before Longarm
so much as touched her, the nipples stood out hard and
firm. Her breathing had become ragged; she was so hot he
was afraid she might burst into flame and burn down half of
central Dwyer.

"Do you . . . ," she turned suddenly shy, "do you like
what you see?"

He smiled. "I like what I see just fine, Helen."

She giggled. "So do I. Let me help you out of those
clothes."

He had already removed his coat and laid it on the bed.
Helen picked it up and carefully hung it in the wardrobe,
then returned to him and unknotted his string tie, unbut-
toned his vest and his shirt—she seemed surprised at the
sight of the derringer that had to come out of his vest
pocket to free one end of the watch chain that stretched
from pocket to pocket—and unbuckled first the gunbelt,
which she placed on the washstand, and then his trousers.

Again she knelt, reaching up to very carefully and slowly
unbutton his trousers.

"Oh, my," she whispered hoarsely when she uncov-
ered Longarm's cock. "It's beautiful. And . . . big. Oh, my."

Helen gently stroked the swollen object in question and
peeled the foreskin back away from the dark, bulbous head.

"Oh, my," she repeated and, leaning forward, first pressed
the warmth of Longarm's prick against her cheek, then took
it into her mouth.

She pulled back far enough to say, "Lovely," then resumed rolling the head around and around within her mouth.

Longarm placed his hand lightly on the back of Helen's

head and let her enjoy herself—it was not exactly unpleasant for him either—for several minutes, until he had to speak up and say, "If you don't quit that, pretty damn soon you are gonna have you a mouthful of cum, lady."

Helen looked up at him and grinned. "Good. I haven't tasted a man in ever so long. Would you mind?"

"Mind? Hell no, I won't mind. Go right ahead an' enjoy yourself."

She returned to the pursuit of her pleasure, taking his cock back into her mouth and rolling her tongue around the head, then sucking him deep into her mouth.

Longarm could feel the pressure of his juices rise near to the point of boiling over. He grabbed a handful of Helen's hair and yanked her face hard onto his cock, driving himself deep into her throat and exploding there, flooding the woman with his semen.

He quivered with effort and with pleasure and held himself inside her for long moments while Helen continued to suck, leaning back every few seconds to swallow and then resume her efforts to pull every last drop from his balls.

He was pretty sure she managed that too.

"Lordy," he breathed at long last, withdrawing from Helen's mouth and lifting her to place her onto her bed.

He nuzzled one of her tits and sucked on the nipple.

"Careful there, cowboy. I'm already so hot you might burn yourself, so please don't start anything you can't finish."

Longarm grinned and gave a playful lick to the tip of a very sensitive nipple. "Give me a couple minutes an' I'll show you what I can finish, that an' then some."

Helen laughed and pulled him hard against her tit.

The woman damn near smothered him with overheated flesh.

He really did not mind.

Chapter 20

Longarm woke early, to find Helen already awake and lying on her side, eyes wide open, just looking at him.

"Is something wrong?" he asked.

"No, not at all. I'm just enjoying having you here in my bed," she said.

He smiled. "My pleasure, believe me." He yawned and stretched a little, enjoying the feel of her warm body pressed close against his. "Tell me about yourself, pretty lady."

Helen blushed. "I wish I was pretty."

"You are," he assured her and with a grin added, "A mighty good fuck too."

"Do you mean that?"

"I do," he said.

"I don't . . . I can't really tell. Until Cory died, he was the only man I was ever in my life with and since then there haven't been but two, not counting you."

"Trust me. You're good." He stretched again, luxuriating in the warm bed and the handsome woman. He idly played with her right tit and asked, "You were happy with him?"

"Very. Cory was a good man and I loved him from the

time we were kids. We came here and built a little house and he ran the saloon and I tended to the home. Then he was killed. It seemed silly for me to keep that house all for myself. Besides, I had memories there that I didn't want haunting me, so I moved into what had been my storeroom here and sold the house. I'm glad I did it. But it gets lonely sometimes." She leaned forward and kissed him. "It's a pleasure to wake up and hear a man's breathing."

He laughed. "Is that a polite way t' say that I was snoring?"

Helen smiled and shrugged, then she slapped him on the chest and said, "I have to open up soon. Can I fix you breakfast first?"

"No," he said, "but you can roll over on your back an' open those legs o' yours. I woke up hard an' think I know how to put that to good use."

It did not take much persuading. In fact the lady required no persuasion at all. She quickly opened herself to him, giving back as good as she got with thrusts and moans, clutching him hard with arms and legs alike.

When they were done, Helen insisted on pouring some water into the basin and washing his cock and balls. With a smile she said, "So you won't be sticky all day. Change your mind about that breakfast?" she offered.

"No, I don't think so. But I hope I'd be welcome to come back for another roll in your hay sometime."

"Anytime," she said.

He dressed quickly and carefully settled the .45 at his waist. He liked to be precise about the placement of the Colt. Just in case he needed to get to it in a hurry.

When he was done, Longarm kissed Helen good-bye and slipped out the back door into a trash-strewn alley rather than be obvious about leaving her place when she was just opening her doors to business. He did not want to ruin the lady's reputation, after all.

He emerged from the alley onto a side street and walked over to the lone café, which now had opened for the day.

The place quite understandably was full, customers crowding the tables until there were only two chairs open. Longarm approached one of them. "Mind if I join you fellas?"

The three men already seated at that table barely looked up. "Sure thing, Marshal," one said, waving in the general direction of the vacant chair.

Longarm sat and tilted his Stetson back from his forehead. "Seems you boys already know who I am. An' you would be . . . ?"

The man who had spoken left off chewing for a moment and said, "I'm Cullen Tifton. These here are Kurt . . . he's the ugly one there on the left," a comment that brought a wide grin from the gentleman in question, "and Karl Biederman. They're krauts."

"*Deutsch*," Karl corrected.

"Right. Krauts," Tifton said with a chuckle. Longarm gathered these three were friends of long standing.

"Kurt and Karl raise chickens. They butcher cockerels and sell eggs too, of course. I raise the grain they feed to their chickens and I run some hogs in the brakes. We all of us farm just south of town where the valley spreads out some. It's good country."

"So I noticed on the drive up here from Casper," Longarm said.

"You're here about the range war, I suppose," Tifton said.

"Aye, so I am. What can you tell me about the trouble that's brewing?" Longarm asked.

Karl piped up. "Dem Meskins, they crazy sons bitches. Try to steal our birds." He turned his head and feigned spitting. "Bastards. Dey come back, I shoot their asses. Got me a shotgun. Load it with salt and shoot der asses, *ja*, I vill."

"Do you know anything about the Mexicans threatening the Basques?" Longarm asked.

"Way I heard it," Tifton said, "it was the Basques saying they were going to fight to keep the Mexicans' goats off their graze."

Longarm thought for a moment and asked, "Mind telling me where you heard the Basques wanted to start a fight?"

"Common knowledge," Tifton said, "but I can't say as I remember where I heard it. Around town, I guess."

"You?" Longarm asked the Biederman brothers.

"I do not remember this," the one on the left said. Longarm could not remember whether that would be Karl or Kurt.

"They say the Meskin goats eat too much grass. The Basque sheep need that, eh?" the other added.

"It's open range," Longarm said.

Tifton shrugged. "They want to keep it all for themselves. So do the Mexicans. I say let them kill each other off if that's what they want."

"No," Kurt said. "They buy our egg. Their money is good."

"I just don't like the idea of foreigners . . . no offense, boys . . . of foreigners coming in here and making trouble for the rest of us."

"Well, that's why I'm here," Longarm said. He looked up at the waiter who had stopped beside his chair.

"We got eggs and spuds and fried pork. It's that or porridge," the waiter said.

"I'll have the eggs and stuff," Longarm told him. "And

coffee. I need my coffee. About a gallon of it just for starters."

"Coming right up. I'll bring the coffee right away and the rest of it soon."

Tifton and the Biederman brothers had already returned to their meals, and Longarm soon joined them in that pursuit.

Chapter 21

Longarm passed through the little gate in front of Sheriff Tyler's house and stepped up onto the porch. "Mornin', John."

"Good morning, Longarm," Tyler said over the rim of a coffee cup. "You surely are quiet. I didn't even hear you come in last night. Didn't hear you leave this morning either."

Longarm laughed. But did not elaborate. He did not want to shame Helen Birch by starting any speculation about where he spent the previous night.

"Are you learning anything?"

"Not very damn much," Longarm said, settling into the comfortable rocker close to Tyler's chair.

"Would you like some breakfast? I'm sure we have some pork chops left over, and Nell could cook you some eggs."

"I'm fine," Longarm said. "Just finished breakfast over to the café. I wanted to hear what folks are saying in town."

"Coffee then?" Tyler asked.

Longarm shook his head. "I'm fine. Really."

"Did you hear anything interesting?"

"Just what you've heard, I'm sure. That folks are expect-

ing a fight. Opinions seem to differ about who's gonna start
it. Mostly they're expecting someone to, it don't hardly
matter who."

Longarm rocked back in the chair and pulled out a cheroot. He nipped the twist off with his teeth and spat it into
his palm, then tossed it into the bushes beside the porch
before fishing out a match and using that to light his cigar.

"What I need," he mused, "is some way to talk to those
Mexican goatherders. I couldn't find none o' them as speaks
English, and you could put my Spanish into your vest
pocket an' have room left over."

"I might have the answer for that," Tyler offered. "Do
you remember the young man at the livery?"

"Anthony? Of course I do," Longarm said.

"Anthony comes from the south of Texas. Someplace
along the Rio Bravo, though I forget the name of it. I've
heard him dickering with the goatherds about this or that.
The boy speaks Spanish like he was born to it. Why don't
you ask him to ride along with you and talk to some of
those fellows?"

"I will, John. Thanks."

"I just wish I could be out there doing what the good
people of McConnell County are paying me for." He
scowled at his own splinted and heavily wrapped leg like it
had deliberately offended him. "Miserable damn cayuse,"
he mumbled.

Longarm stood. "Reckon I'll step over to the livery an'
see can I hire Anthony for that piece of work."

"If there is anything I can do . . ." Tyler sounded hope-
ful that there might be, but Longarm could think of nothing
the man might be able to do that would be helpful. Not
at the moment anyway. Perhaps he could come up with
something later, though, if for no other reason than to let
the local sheriff feel that he was being useful.

"You've already been a big help," Longarm assured him.

Tyler grunted his disbelief and took a swallow of his coffee.

The livery was empty save for the livestock stabled there, and there was no note to indicate where Anthony DeCaro had gotten to. Still, Dwyer was not so big a town that a man could get lost there. Longarm tracked DeCaro down in Samuel Johnson's mercantile. The young hostler was arranging for the import of a load of horseshoe nails.

"Where do those have to come from?" Longarm asked.

"Cheyenne," DeCaro told him.

"Pretty much everything has to come up from Cheyenne," Johnson said. "The railroad, you see. We have goods shipped by rail to Cheyenne then carted up here by bull trains or the smaller items on the stagecoach."

"That makes sense," Longarm said. "Y'know, while I think about it, I have a question for you, Mr. Johnson."

"Sam," the man corrected. "Everyone calls me Sam."

"All right then, Sam. You handle freight orders here, I take it, just like you handle the stagecoach business?"

"That's right, I do."

"Then do you happen to know how the Basques are armed? I noticed a lot of modern repeating rifles in that camp."

"Is this an official inquiry?" Johnson asked. "Because I shouldn't tell you if it isn't. Privacy and all that."

"It's official," Longarm said.

"All right then. Yes, I handled the freight order for that. Two cases of rifles at twenty-eight dollars each . . . I made a fair profit on those, if I do say so . . . and four cases of .44-40 ammunition. All of it prepaid by a gentleman named Wisner. I don't know anything about him, though, or why he would be arming those Basques."

"They work for Wisner," Longarm said.

"That explains it then."

"And the Mexicans?" Longarm asked. "Have they armed themselves too?"

"Not through me, they haven't. I sell them some shotgun shells and loose powder and percussion caps but nothing in any volume," Johnson said.

"They haven't loaded up with firearms the way the Basques have," DeCaro put in. "They just have what they normally carry to keep predators away from their goats."

"So if it came to a war, the Basques would likely win?" Longarm asked.

DeCaro frowned in thought then said, "Maybe. There's more Mexicans than there are Basques, but the Basques are better armed. The Mexican boys are used to fighting. They've had more than enough of it down their way. They can handle themselves if it comes to a scrap. I don't know about the Basques. Don't know anything about how it is where they come from. In my opinion I think it could go either way."

"What about you, Sam? What do you think?"

"Don't ask me, Marshal. I stay strictly neutral about things like this."

Longarm thought about saying *And you'll sell arms to either side as long as you get your profit on the deal*, but he put a brake on his tongue. Instead he said, "Anthony, I'd like to have a word with you when you're done here."

"Sure thing, Marshal."

"I'll wait on one o' those handsome benches over by the courthouse," Longarm said.

"Fine. I'll meet you there. Won't be but a minute and I'll be finished with my business."

Longarm touched the brim of his Stetson toward Johnson, then turned and headed across the street toward the McConnell County Courthouse and the privacy of the public square, where no one was apt to be close when he spoke with DeCaro.

Chapter 22

Longarm scarcely had time to finish a cheroot before De-Caro showed up and sat on the bench beside him.

"Sorry if I kept you waiting too long," the young hostler said.

Longarm grinned. "Not at all. I sat here an' watched some fine-looking women out for their daily shopping."

"Dwyer does seem to have some uncommonly good-looking women," DeCaro said, "but all the really good-looking ones are married."

"Now, that, son, is a damned shame."

"What is it you wanted to see me about, Marshal?"

"I want to hire you, Anthony. Sheriff Tyler tells me you speak Spanish right well. Is that so?"

DeCaro shyly glanced down toward the toes of his boots and said, "I wouldn't claim to be any sort of flash at it. For sure I don't know anything fancy or flowery, but I expect I did grow up with it. I was raised down in Piedras Negras, if you know where that is."

Longarm nodded. "I been there."

"Yeah, well, me and my pals was over on the Mexican

side of the river about as much as we were on the American side. Just raising Cain and like that. Nothing serious. We had Mexican friends, about as many as there were Anglos in our crowd. We all pretty much spoke whatever seemed handy at the time, so I can pretty much hold my own with it. Just what are you needing Spanish for, if you don't mind me asking?"

"I need to talk with these Mex goatherds, Anthony. I'd rather head off a war than step into the middle o' one. Figure I ought to get a look at their side o' things before I go to doing anything dramatic."

"I can help you with that, Marshal."

"The federal government will allow me to pay you a dollar a day for interpreting services. Will that be all right?"

"Marshal, I'd do it for nothing if it will help keep this county quiet."

"A dollar a day it is then. And you can call me Longarm." He smiled. "All my friends do." He extended his hand to the handsome young man and they shook on the deal. "We'll start out first thing tomorrow."

"There's only one thing wrong with that," DeCaro said with a grin.

Longarm raised his eyebrows. "Hmm?"

"You're riding my horse."

"I can get him back to you and swap you for . . ."

"Marshal . . . Longarm, I mean . . . I'm just funning you. I got plenty of decent horses to pick from. I'll come by Sheriff Tyler's house right after breakfast tomorrow."

Longarm nodded. "Pack a lunch. Those goatherds are scattered all through the valley. It'll likely take us a while to chase them down."

"I'll be there." Anthony DeCaro seemed pleased as he stood to head back toward his livery stable.

"One more thing," Longarm said, stopping him.

"Yes, Marshal?"

Longarm fingered his chin, dark with several days' growth of beard. "Where can I find a barber hereabouts?"

Chapter 23

Dwyer's barber was a gentleman named Bert—Longarm did not get the man's last name—who was riding the borderline between middle-aged and just plain elderly. He was tall, bald, and frail, but he seemed to know what he was doing. Longarm sat patiently eavesdropping while the three customers before him received their trims and their shaves, until he was called to the chair.

"What can I do for you, Marshal?"

"Shave an' a trim, I reckon."

Bert nodded, draped a striped sheet over Longarm, and brought a hot, slightly damp towel out of the warmer oven attached to a very small stove. He deftly wrapped the towel around Longarm's lower face.

"Damn that feels good," Longarm said.

Bert smiled and began slapping a razor back and forth across a strop. When he was satisfied with the razor, he laid it on top of a clean towel and picked up his soap cup and brush, expertly whipping up a lather. He took the towel away from Longarm's face and began applying the lather.

"I'll let this set and soften your beard while I give you

that trim," he said, continuing to brush the lather on.

"That's fine," Longarm said. "I'm in no rush." He nodded to a gent who came into the shop. Bert seemed to be doing a good business here. But then he was the only barber in town.

Bert snipped at the back of Longarm's head and carefully trimmed around his ears before saying, "You should be about ready now," and taking up his razor. He leaned forward to make the first stroke but was interrupted by the dull, booming sound of gunshots, two of them very close together, from somewhere nearby.

Longarm came out of the barber chair as quickly as if he were the one being shot at. He flung the striped sheet aside and headed for the door, unmindful of the lather that still coated his cheeks and neck.

He ran out without bothering to grab his Stetson off the rack near Bert's door.

In the wide street that fronted the courthouse he saw trouble.

There were two men. Or rather one man and what used to be another.

The one who was standing was small and dark and ragged. He held a double-barreled shotgun and wore a stunned and fearful expression, as if he did not completely understand what it was that he had just done.

And what it was that he had done was to damned near cut another man in two with those two gunshots.

That man lay sprawled in the dirt eight or ten feet away from the shooter, his chest and belly ripped open and turned into an exposed mass of blood, lungs, and guts. A shiny new Winchester rifle was on the ground at his side.

Revolver in hand, Longarm carefully approached the shooter. "Don't be makin' no sudden moves there, partner," he said in a low, soothing voice as if speaking to a nervous horse. He held the .45 aimed at the man's midsection while he reached out and plucked the shotgun away from the fellow. The man offered no resistance, in fact seemed not to so much as notice what Longarm had done.

Longarm lay the shotgun on the ground and turned the man around. He shoved his revolver back into its holster and took handcuffs out of his back pocket, quickly snapping the steel onto the man's wrists. He bent and retrieved the shotgun then glanced toward the dead man.

The barber, who apparently did double duty as Dwyer's doctor and its undertaker, was kneeling beside the recently deceased. Others were beginning to gather close as well now that the danger was over.

"Can anybody tell me what happened here?" Longarm asked in a loud voice.

"Yeah, I can," a young man wearing bib overalls and a denim cap said. He stepped forward. "These two were arguing, sir. Near as I could tell they were speaking different languages and neither one of them seemed to understand what the other was saying. They got real loud and angry. This one here," he pointed toward the dead man, "started shaking his fist in that one's face. Then that one," he indicated the survivor, "just up and cut loose on him. It was over just like that." He snapped his fingers. "It was pretty ugly, Marshal. It was just plain murder."

"This guy didn't point his rifle or threaten this one here?" Longarm asked.

The young man shrugged and said, "Damned if I'd know what either one of them said. All I could tell is that they both sounded pretty well pissed off shouting at each other like that, but I don't know about what."

"All right, thanks." Longarm nudged his prisoner into

motion and guided him around to the back of the courthouse and down the steps to the sheriff's office and jail. He
pushed the unprotesting prisoner close to the door, trans-
ferred the shotgun to the crook of his arm, and fumbled in
his pockets for the key the clerk had given him.

He kept a wary eye on the prisoner while he got the door
open and took him inside and straight through to one of the
two jail cells.

Only one of the cells had a small window to admit air
and a little daylight. Longarm propped the shotgun against
the wall then put the shooter in the cell that had no window.
He had to look around for the key to lock the cell. He found
it hanging on a nail in the other room. Before he locked the
man in, he carefully frisked him and took a folding pocket-
knife out of the man's pocket.

"Got anything to say for yourself?" he asked.

The shooter's expression did not change, and Longarm
got the impression the man scarcely knew he was there. He
seemed to be in a state of shock.

Longarm left him to get over it on his own and went
back out to the office. His face felt drawn and uncomfortable from the shaving lather that was beginning to dry on it,
but he had no towel to wipe it away or any water to wash it
off. That would just have to wait.

He retrieved the shotgun and broke it open. Both shells
had been discharged. He pulled them out and took a look.
They were—or rather had been—buckshot loads. It was no
wonder they had done such damage. Two loads of buck
fired at close range? The dead man might as well have been
standing in front of a canon.

He went outside, carefully locking the door behind him
lest there be some of the dead man's friends in town who
wanted a chance to visit with the shooter, then Longarm
returned to the barbershop. The shave would just have to

wait, but he wanted a towel to get the lather off his face, and he wanted to reclaim his hat and coat. Walking bareheaded in the sunshine felt vaguely uncomfortable; he was not used to it.

Chapter 24

Stetson back where it belonged, Longarm walked over to the livery. He found Anthony DeCaro with a shovel in hand, cleaning out the barn stalls.

"I need your translating skills, Anthony. At least I think I do."

"You *think* you do?" DeCaro responded.

"Well, I don't know for sure that this fella is a Mexican, but I think he probably is."

DeCaro set his shovel aside and took out a bandanna that he used to mop the sweat off his face. "What fellow would that be, Longarm?"

"Guy I got in the jail. He's in there for murder?"

DeCaro's eyebrows went up. "I don't know that we've ever had a murder in Dwyer. Who is he and who did he kill?"

"Anthony, I don't have an answer to either one of them questions. That's why I'm hoping you can talk to him. See if we can make some sense of this."

"All right. I'll be glad to help if I can, Longarm." De-

Caro brushed himself off a little, then headed for the court-house and the sheriff's office in the basement there.

When Longarm and DeCaro got there, the door was standing open, and for a moment Longarm feared a lynch mob had broken in. He motioned for DeCaro to stay back and, revolver in hand, cautiously approached the door.

Inside he found Sheriff John Tyler seated at his desk, crutches propped against the wall.

"I heard the gunshots," Tyler said, "and I could see all the commotion in the street. Saw the shooting to begin with, for that matter. I grabbed my crutches and started down here. I saw you had it under control, Longarm, but I wanted to be here anyway."

"Nell is gonna be pissed off at you, y'know," Longarm said, "coming all this way on your crutches. You'll wear yourself out." He grinned. "That's bad enough, but she might blame me for not headin' you off."

"She'll get over it. The point is, it is my job to keep the law in this town. I can't do it if I'm sitting on my front porch all the time."

"You've seen the prisoner then, I take it," Longarm said.

Tyler nodded. "I tried talking to him, but that didn't seem to do much good. I don't know as he understood a single word I said."

"That's why I went to fetch Anthony here." Longarm inclined his head in DeCaro's direction. "The prisoner looks to be Mexican. Maybe Anthony can get some sense outa him. I sure as hell hope so because I'm pretty sure the fella he killed was one of them Basque sheepherders." Longarm took a deep breath. "John, this here could be the spark that sets off the range war we've been worryin' about. When the Basques find out about it, it ain't gonna be good."

"They probably know by now," Tyler said. "A horseman galloped past me as I was working my way down here. He was headed up the valley, and my bet is that he was going to inform the friends of that dead man."

"Then hell on the hoof could be headed our way right now," Longarm said.

Chapter 25

Hell on the hoof, he had said. It arrived about an hour and a half later. "Hello, Eli," Longarm said as the visitor entered the sheriff's office.

John Tyler sat behind his desk and Longarm lounged in a chair that had been pulled up beside the desk, both men facing the door that was the only way in or out of the basement facility. They both had sawed-off shotguns lying across their laps, guns taken down from the rack on the back wall of Tyler's office. Both guns were loaded with the same heavy buckshot loads that had virtually cut a Basque in two earlier.

"You know what I came for," Eli Cruikshank said in a soft Texas drawl.

Tyler nodded. Longarm said, "Sit down, Eli. Hear what we got t' say."

Cruikshank turned a chair around and straddled it as if it were a horse and he was in a saddle.

Longarm smiled. "I'd appreciate it, friend, if you'd keep your hands out from behind the back o' that chair where we can see them. Just to make me feel better, if you know what I mean."

"Sorry," Cruikshank said, sounding like he was anything but sorry. "I never thought."

"Right," Longarm said, not meaning that either.

"The thing is," Tyler said, "Julio Altameira is in custody and under arrest on a charge of murder. He will be arraigned before Judge Thompson when that worthy gentleman gets here. He will be tried. He will be found guilty . . . there is no doubt about that as I witnessed the murder myself . . . and he will receive whatever penalty the law imposes. My guess is that the man will be hanged, but that isn't up to me." Tyler leaned forward and hardened his voice when he said, "It is not up to you or to the Basques either."

"The way I heard it," Cruikshank said, "that man just cut Estevan Corrales down, shot him in cold blood."

"That's true enough," Longarm said. "The two of 'em met on the street. There's no way to know what your man Corrales was thinking, but Altameira admits to being scared of him. Corrales was carryin' a rifle. Altameira had his shotgun. The two got to jawing at each other. Neither one of 'em could understand a word the other was saying. Corrales kept getting closer an' talking louder, and Altameira kept getting scareder an' scareder, an' the next thing you know there was the shootin'. Altameira claims it was near to being an accident, that he didn't really intend to shoot Corrales."

"An accident." Cruikshank scoffed. "Shot him by accident. With both fucking barrels."

Longarm shrugged. "I'm only tellin' you what the man said."

"There's people out there that aren't going to like this," Cruikshank said.

"There's people in here that don't like it," Longarm said.

"Now it is up to the law to find justice for that dead man," Sheriff Tyler said. "The law, Cruikshank."

"Can I see this prisoner of yours?" Cruikshank asked.

"If you will surrender your weapons before you are taken in front of him, yes, you may," Tyler said.

"Give up my guns?"

"Exactly," Tyler said with a nod.

"And I'll be right beside you to protect you if the Mexican goes for your throat," Longarm added.

"I don't surrender my guns to any man," Cruikshank said in a gentle but firm tone.

"Then you do not interview the prisoner," Tyler said just as firmly.

"So what should I tell my people?"

"Tell them the man that killed their friend is in jail. Tell them the man will be tried all legal and proper and most likely hanged for what he done," Longarm said.

"Can they watch the hanging?" Cruikshank asked.

"If it happens," Tyler said, "it will be a public hanging."

"I don't know that that will satisfy them, it being uncertain and sometime in the far distant future," Cruikshank said. "Their culture is different from ours. They figure it to be blood for blood and no waiting for it to be dragged out in a court system they don't really understand."

"They are living in our culture now," Tyler told him. "They will abide by our law."

"Either that or they'll find themselves in a cell right alongside of Altameira," Longarm said.

"Maybe they will accept that. Maybe they won't," Cruikshank said. "I will tell them what you say but I make no promises, not if I don't know for certain sure that I can keep them." He glanced toward the door leading back to the cells, but he made no move in that direction. "Thank you for the information," he said.

Cruikshank stood, his right hand coming very close to his holstered revolver when he got up from the chair.

Neither Tyler nor Longarm rose with him. And neither let his hand stray far from the hammer of the double-barreled shotgun he was holding.

"Explain it to them," Tyler said.

"I'll do that," Cruikshank responded. He touched the brim of his hat, nodded, and quietly left the sheriff's office.

"Whew," Longarm said when Cruikshank had gone. "Reckon I can breathe somewhat better now."

"Me too," Tyler said with a shudder. "I think from now on one of us needs to be sitting down here with a shotgun handy. I've never lost a prisoner to a lynching and I don't want to start now."

Longarm nodded. "Yes, sir." He lighted a cheroot and said, "I'll sleep here tonight. Meantime I'm gonna go finish that shave I didn't quite get this morning."

Chapter 26

Longarm did not like the noise he was hearing coming from Rosie's saloon, the one that catered to the Basque shepherds and to locals who were more interested in getting laid than in simply drinking and playing cards or billiards.

When Longarm stepped inside to take a look, shotgun still in hand, the entire place became suddenly silent. He walked to the bar, the crowd of patrons—there must have been a score of them—parting before him like the Red Sea parting at the exodus.

"Beer, Marshal?" the bartender asked.

Longarm nodded, laid a dime down, and faced away from the bar, leaning his back against it and holding the stubby sawed-off in the crook of his left arm. He slipped his right thumb behind his belt buckle, which put it just two or three inches from the butt of his Colt. "Gentlemen," he said to no one in particular.

One of the Basques stepped forward and rattled off something in his own tongue. Longarm was just as happy that he did not understand a single word of what became a rather long diatribe, no doubt discussing Longarm's fore-bears, mental deficiencies, and sexual habits.

After a minute or two of that, Longarm turned, picked up his beer, and saluted the complaining Basque with his mug before taking a long, throat cleansing swallow.

He looked across a sea of dark hair and floppy hats but found no sign of Eli Cruikshank. That was probably just as well, he decided. If Eli had been there, he would more than likely have wanted to translate what the loudmouthed Basque was saying, and then Longarm would have felt honor bound to be pissed off by the whole thing.

He finished his beer and asked the bartender, "Can you understand what they're saying?"

The barman shook his head. "Not a word of it, Marshal."

Longarm did not know if the man was lying to him or not. He had no choice but to let it go, however.

The Basque finally shut up. Longarm saluted him with his beer mug again and walked out of Rosie's.

It occurred to him as he left to wonder if there was a Rosie somewhere in Dwyer. Or perhaps the name referred to the owner's lost love somewhere.

Not that it mattered.

With a sigh, he returned to the barbershop, where he found that Bert was still occupied with the corpse of the recently departed.

This just was *not* Custis Long's day.

Chapter 27

Longarm's whiskers were just long enough to reach the itching stage. He either had to get a shave soon or resign himself to another three or four days of damned near unbearable itching. Bert was off tending to a corpse, however, and Longarm did not want to go back to Tyler's house to fetch his own razor. It would not be seemly for him to be there alone with Nell while John was camped out inside the sheriff's office watching over Julio Altameira.

Nope. It just was not his day.

Still, life crawls forward whether we want it to or not, whether things are turning out the way we wish or not. Longarm belched, lighted a cheroot, and walked over to the café for an early lunch.

He ate, then had them fix up a basket of biscuits and ham to carry over to Tyler, who was parked in his office with a shotgun across his lap. Longarm was behind the courthouse, close to the stairs leading down into the basement, when a commotion caught his attention.

Someone was shouting—cussing, he guessed by the sound of it—at the front of the big stone building.

Longarm set Tyler's lunch down on the top step and walked around to the front to see what the trouble was.

He grimaced with displeasure when he saw a knot of six Mexican goatherds confronting two Basque shepherds. All of the men were armed. A pair of shaggy, black-and-white dogs accompanied the goatherds, while the Basques held a large brown cur on a rope leash.

The men were jawing at one another, and the Basques' dog was straining at his restraint, ready to do battle with the other dogs. Or, for all Longarm knew, the animal was ready to fight the Mexicans.

"Shit," he mumbled aloud. "This could be the start o' that war."

He trotted across the ragged and weedy courthouse lawn to the benches where the men were standing and snapping at one another.

Longarm was about to say something to them when one of the Mexicans spoke and his dogs lunged for the brown that belonged to the Basques.

Within seconds the brown dog had one black dog at its throat and another biting and snarling at its flank.

The Basque who had hold of the brown dog's leash shouted and jumped back, letting his dog go so it could defend itself.

For a moment the two groups of men were too intent on watching their dogs fight to pay attention to each other.

Each group began loudly exhorting their animals.

The dogs meanwhile were tangled in a barking, snapping, snarling whirl of dust and flying fur.

Despite being outnumbered two to one, the brown dog appeared to be getting the best of the fight. It shook a black-and-white dog off and laid open a hind leg of the other Mexican dog, then attacked the first black-and-white head-on, driving the dog into the dirt and taking a grip on that one's throat.

The Mexicans saw their dogs down and bleeding, possibly dying. One of them raised his rifle and shot the brown dog in the body.

Instantly the Basques had their rifles up and appeared to be ready to shoot too.

Chapter 28

Longarm charged in between the two groups—a move that he later, when he had time to think about it, found to be remarkably stupid, considering that he was stepping between two armed and volatile camps—yelling and motioning with the barrels of the sawed-off for them to put their guns down and back off. Amazingly, they did.

"You," he said, motioning to the Mexicans, "go. Vamoose. *Andale.* Whatever the fuck those words are. Anyhow, git!" He pointed toward Doris's saloon and made hand motions to shoo the men in that direction.

One of the black-and-white dogs was dead, its throat ripped out by the brown, but the other was only bleeding from a deep gash in its hind leg. That one likely would live, even be able to return to work if someone sewed the wound closed. The surviving dog was picked up by one of the Mexicans, who draped it over his shoulder while another man stanched the wound with a handful of dust and a wrap of his bandanna.

The brown dog was still alive but barely so. The Basques shot furious glares—but only looks at this point—at the retreating Mexicans. They knelt beside their dying dog, and one of them dropped into the dirt of the street and pulled the animal's head into his lap. The dog licked his hand twice and then died. Longarm could see tears on the man's cheeks.

The other Basque stood and took a fresh grip on his rifle.

"I wouldn't do that, old son," Longarm warned.

The Basque glanced once at the stern expression on Longarm's face, shivered, and let his rifle drop, muzzle down. After a few minutes the two Basques picked up their dead dog and walked away.

Longarm looked up at the imposing McConnell County Courthouse and pondered what the hell he could do to keep warfare from breaking out around it.

He stood there for perhaps five minutes before he squared his shoulders and with a grunt set off at a rapid pace.

He went to Doris's saloon and marched inside. The Mexicans who were drinking and talking there turned quiet and sullen at his appearance among them.

"Who's the owner here?" he demanded of the man behind the bar.

"In the back," the man said, inclining his head in that direction.

"Get him," Longarm snapped.

"It's a her not a him," the barman said.

"Fine. So get her. An' do it damn quick."

"What makes you think I'll . . ." The bartender shut his mouth when he saw the deadly cold stare he received from the lawman. "Uh, yes, sir. Right away."

Longarm did not have long to wait. Seconds after the bartender disappeared into the back, a woman emerged in his place behind the long bar. She was on the cloudy side of middle age, with her hair done into a tight bun and wearing a throat-high, long-sleeved charcoal-colored dress. Her face was marred by the sort of tracks left by a past bout with a pox of some sort. She did not look particularly welcoming.

"What do you want, Marshal?" Her voice was rough enough to cut wood.

"I'm closing you down," he said.

"What?"

"You heard me. By the authority vested in me, I am hereby declaring this saloon closed."

"Why . . . you can't do any such of a thing."

"The hell you say," he replied. "I've just done it."

"How long do you want me to close?" she asked.

"Until I tell you otherwise," he told her. "Until we can figure out a way t' keep these Meskins an' Basques from killing each other."

"I don't have anything to do with that," the woman rasped.

"Maybe not direct you don't," Longarm agreed, "but the whiskey an' beer you're servin' in here sure helps t' fire 'em up. So I'm shutting your doors for the duration. I'll come back and let you know when you can open up again."

"The town council will have something to say about this," she snarled. "Then we shall see about this supposed authority of yours."

"Until then you'd damn sure better close down and stay shut," Longarm told her.

Without any further argument, he spun on his heels and marched out again—on his way to Rosie's to deliver the same message to keep the Basques from getting liquored up with false bravery.

When he was done there, with much the same unhappy compliance, he returned to the rear of the courthouse to finally retrieve John Tyler's lunch.

The basket was where he had left it. The food was not.

But some very contented town dogs were lolling in the shade not very far away.

No, sir, it just plain was not his day, Longarm figured, as he turned and headed back to the café to get the lunch basket refilled.

Chapter 29

"Where's my dish towel, damn you?"

"I lost it."

"Then you'll damn well pay for a new one."

Longarm sighed. "Put it on my bill."

"Damn right I will."

"Now, make me another lunch an' load it in this basket, will you. The first one got the same kinda lost as your dish towel."

The café owner grunted. "Give me a minute. And this time don't lose the damn towel."

"I promise," Longarm assured the man. Five minutes later he walked past a group of sullen Mexican goatherds, descended the stairs to the courthouse basement, and rapped twice on the door before he opened it.

Sheriff Tyler was behind his desk with a shotgun aimed squarely at the doorway. It would take a concerted effort for anyone to get inside, and people would have to die for the task to be accomplished. Longarm doubted that the Mexicans were so attached to their compadre Altameira that they were willing to risk death in an attempt to free him.

"I brought you some lunch," Longarm said, hefting the basket. "Actually I brought you two lunches. Some town dogs got the first one." He filled Tyler in on what had taken place on the street earlier.

"Figured it ain't a good idea for either crowd to be gettin' liquored up today, so I shut down both Doris's and Rosie's places. Told 'em I'd let them know when they can open up again."

"You know, don't you, that you have no authority to do such a thing," Tyler said.

Longarm grinned. "D'you know, that's the same thing they told me at both them places."

"Yes, but you really don't."

Longarm shrugged. "They're gonna take it up with the town council, whenever that will be. If the town council says they can reopen, I'll appeal to whatever judge rides this circuit. That should hold things off plenty long enough for us to get this bullshit resolved, one way or the other."

"Dogs are important to those people," Tyler said. "I'm surprised they didn't start the ball there in the street this morning."

"They come awful close, John. Awful close." Longarm set the food basket on the desk in front of Tyler.

"Thanks, but Nell brought my lunch down to me."

"Shit, I shoulda thought of that." Longarm peeled back the towel laid over the top of the basket, reached in, and brought out a slice of ham and a biscuit. He carefully separated the biscuit into top and bottom halves, put the slice of ham in between and leaned back while he enjoyed a second lunch himself. He damned sure was not going to try to return the lunch to the café. Not after those dogs carried the first one off.

"What I can't figure out, John," he said, crumbs of flaky biscuit trickling down onto his vest, "is why these two bunches are so set on fightin' one another. It ain't like there isn't grass an' water enough for both of 'em in this valley. You would think they could get along, no more than there are of them and as much grass as there is up there." He sighed. "Maybe Anthony and me can get a handle on it all when we ride up there tomorrow morning."

Longarm finished the basket lunch then stood. "I'm gonna go see if that barber is done fooling around with the mortal remains of . . . what was his name? Corrales? . . . so's I can get me a shave before I scratch my damn chin bloody. Then, if you don't mind, I'll come back here an' bunk down in that vacant cell back there, so I'll be able to take over the guard duty from you this evening. If anything happens, give a shout. I'll come running."

"I don't really expect any trouble," Tyler said, "but it's good to know you will be back there anyway."

Longarm picked up the now empty basket and headed for yet another trip to the café.

Chapter 30

Longarm returned to the jail feeling considerably less itchy and smelling of Pinaud Clubman. The goatherds and one dog were still gathered at the front of the courthouse, but they were quiet. Sullen but quiet. He considered running them off with the threat of loitering charges—if there was such a thing in Dwyer, and if there was not, there should be—but that might only make things worse. At least if they were that close by, he knew where they were and what they were up to. If he sent them somewhere else, there was no telling what trouble they might get into.

He settled for letting them get a good look at him and at the McConnell County deputy's badge he had pinned to his coat. The badge more than made up for his lack of Spanish; it spoke volumes in any language.

He stood at the top of the steps down into the sheriff's office for a few moments then went down, rapped lightly on the door, and went inside.

"Everything all right?" Tyler said.

Longarm nodded. "So far so good."

"Are those Mexicans still up there?"

Longarm nodded again.

"Do you want to get Anthony to talk to them?"

"No," Longarm said, "I don't think so. They aren't causing any trouble, really, and I figure they're just there to stay close to their pal Julio. They ain't all worked up in a fury or nothin'. I don't think they got thoughts o' breaking him out or anything. Though I expect they might think of that if they was to get all liquored up. Which is why I shut Doris down. The less they drink, the better off we are."

He yawned and stretched. "If you don't mind, John, I'll go back there to your cells an' lay down. Get a little shut-eye. I'll try an' wake up in time for you to go home and have one of your lady's fine meals. Then you can come back and relieve me in the morning so's Anthony and me can try and make some sense of this feuding an' fussing."

"Go ahead," Tyler said.

"One thing, John. Was I you, I think I'd bolt that door. If they do get worked up and try to bust Altameira out of here, they'll come in a rush."

"All right, Longarm. You have more experience with this sort of thing than I ever want to." Tyler stood and took his shotgun with him while he went to the door and locked it, then slid the bolt closed for that much extra security.

Longarm touched the brim of his Stetson in Tyler's direction then went back to the cells, where Julio Altameira was moping in a corner. If the man was this depressed from being in a county cell, Longarm suspected he would not do well once he got into the brutal confinement of a prison.

Of course the stupid son of a bitch might get lucky and be hanged instead.

With that cheery thought in mind, Longarm removed his hat and coat—but kept the county's shotgun close to hand—and lay down on the hard and too short bunk to get a little sleep while he had the chance.

Later, John Tyler brought him one of Nell's homemade dinners—a huge step up from what Longarm was accustomed to—and he locked up for the night. He then spent a boring evening sitting at Tyler's desk, and about one o'clock he returned to the empty cell to catch some more sleep while he had the chance.

Chapter 31

Longarm woke up with Helen Birch on his mind and a raging hard-on in his britches. He had a thirst that was almost as demanding. The Mexican prisoner in the adjacent cell was sitting on the bunk staring at him, but Longarm did not know if that was because Altameira was afraid of what the lawman might do . . . or if the sorry son of a bitch was in awe of Longarm's tent pole–sized erection.

When Longarm said, "Good morning," the fellow turned his head and pretended he had not been staring.

Longarm left Altameira to his own dark thoughts and went back to his vigil behind John Tyler's desk. Shortly after sunup, the McConnell County sheriff returned to his office. He brought Longarm a plate of breakfast and a pitcher of hot coffee.

"Nell's coffee is a whole lot better than what I make here," Tyler said with a smile, "so I thought I would spare you the experience of drinking mine."

"Thoughtful of you, John," Longarm told him. He walked over to the water bucket, chose a tin mug from the selection hanging there, and poured himself a cup of the wonderfully aromatic beverage, then dug into the spread Nell had sent.

"Y'know, John," he said around a mouthful of sausage and golden brown toast, "that woman of yours would be worth marryin' even if she wasn't pretty as a sunrise. You're a lucky man."

Tyler beamed as if the compliment had been for him and not his wife.

"Are you gonna be all right here today, d'you think?" Longarm asked.

"I'm fine."

"Are those Mexicans still hanging around outside?"

The sheriff shook his head. "Not yet, but it's early. They might show up. That would be bad, but it'd be worse if the Basques come."

"I'm thinkin' if the Basques want to kill Altameira, they won't come in a bunch, John. They'll send Eli Cruikshank to do their blood work. That boy strikes me as bein' real seriously salty. If he comes, don't let him taunt you out of this hole. He can't get you through a closed door, and they can't burn a stone building down over you, so just stay shut inside here till I come back."

"Do you think it could come to that, Longarm?"

"Yes, sir, I do," he answered with a grimace and a nod. Longarm used the last bite of toast to mop up the egg yolk left on his plate, then sat back and rubbed his belly. "Mighty fine, John, thank you. Is there any more of that good coffee left?"

"Plenty," Tyler said, tipping the pitcher over Longarm's cup.

"I'll treat myself to this, then go fetch Anthony and start the day." He shook his head. "I just can't figure why those Mexicans are so set on running the Basques out of here when there's grass and water enough for both. Shit, cattlemen have it in mind that sheep ruin the graze for cows, but there's no such feelings about goats, dammit. Nor the other way around. Sheep and goats can graze side by side and no harm to either. So why pick this fight?"

"Maybe you and Anthony can get some answers today," Tyler said.

"If we're damn lucky," Longarm said, standing and squatting down a few times to get the circulation moving in his legs.

He touched the butt of his Colt to assure himself that the revolver was in the exact spot where he liked it, put his coat on, and reached for his Stetson.

"If you will excuse me, John, I got work t' do."

"I'll guard the fort till you get back. Whoa, wait a minute. Aren't you forgetting something?"

Longarm stopped by the door and looked back at the county sheriff.

"Don't you want to take the shotgun with you?"

Longarm shook his head. "We'll be out in the open today. If anything happens, it'll be at long range."

"A rifle then?"

"Got my own saddle Winchester, thanks. We'll be fine."

"All right then. Good luck."

"Don't forget now. Lock this door and bolt it behind me. Don't let nobody in except for me or Nell."

"Yes, Mother," Tyler said with a grin. "Nobody in but you or Nell. Now quit worrying and go see if you can learn anything from those goatherds."

Longarm left, closing the door behind him. He did not mount the steps, though, until he heard the scrape of the bolt being thrown behind him. Only then did he return to the little barn behind Tyler's house to fetch the dun horse and his gear.

Chapter 32

Anthony DeCaro was saddled and ready when Longarm got to the livery. "Where are we going?" he asked, then swung into his saddle. He was riding a wild-eyed Appaloosa that looked like it had more spirit than sense.

"North," Longarm said. "The Basques are pretty much unified and Eli speaks English, but there's no such luck with the Mexicans. Aside from none of 'em seeming to speak English, them and their goats are scattered all to hell and gone."

"There are two or three of them that have some influence though," DeCaro said.

"You know them?"

DeCaro nodded. "Not well, but . . . yeah. I'd have to say that I know them. They put their horses up with me when they intend to stay overnight with one of Doris's whores."

"Know where to find them now?"

DeCaro grinned and inclined his head toward the north. "Up that way somewheres," he said and added, "Can't be but twenty or so small flocks scattered up that way." He reined his Appaloosa into the road, Longarm following.

The first bunch of goats were within a mile of downtown Dwyer, and several others were grazing not much farther to the north. Those, Longarm figured, would belong to the herdsmen who had gathered outside the jail yesterday. And were very likely to do so again today.

"How do they manage to get away to come into town to drink or make threats to the sheriff?" Longarm asked.

DeCaro turned in his saddle to answer, but before he could do so, the Appaloosa blew up under him, bogging its head with a snort, bowing its broad back, and doing its level best to pitch that human creature off of it.

Longarm reined the dun, as steady as DeCaro had promised, off away from the impromptu rodeo and sat there admiring the young livery owner's ability to stick on board the suddenly crazy animal.

The Appaloosa leaped and twisted. Clods of dirt flew a dozen feet into the air, and dust rose in a brown cloud around the furious horse.

Anthony DeCaro stuck to his saddle like a burr on a dog's butt. This was no rodeo competition and there were no judges watching to award points. The young liveryman hung onto his saddle horn and clung tight with his legs. Longarm suspected he would have grabbed hold with his teeth too if he could have. If nothing else, that would have helped to keep his head from whipping back and forth the way it now was.

The battle went on for what seemed a very long time but surely wasn't. Longarm had time to pull out a cheroot and light it, but the little cigar scarcely built an ash before the fight was over, DeCaro being the uncontested victor.

DeCaro reined the sweating but now calm Appaloosa over beside Longarm on the dun. He was grinning but looked a little the worse for wear. His shirttail was out of his britches, and his hat, while still on his head, was some-what askew.

"Keep that up," Longarm said, "an' you'll be an old man before your time."

DeCaro's grin never faded. "No doubt," he agreed. "My spine feels like a damn accordion as it is. I suppose I really ought to sell this son of a bitch down the road, but he's tough and he's honest, and the truth is that I just plain like him." He laughed. "Damned if I know why though."

"I hope that ain't the horse you were gonna give me if I'd asked for something fast," Longarm said.

DeCaro laughed again. "As a matter of fact, he is."

Longarm leaned down to pat the thick, heavily muscled neck of the little dun horse he had been given instead.

When he leaned low over the dun's neck, he heard the sizzle of a bullet slicing through the air and immediately afterward the solid whack of lead striking dirt.

"Shit!" Longarm yelped as he spurred the dun into a run.

He was already moving before he heard the dull bark of a rifle shot from somewhere to his right.

Anthony DeCaro's Appaloosa was indeed faster than the steady little dun horse. The App proved that as DeCaro quickly caught up with Longarm and passed him.

The young hostler ran ahead for a half mile or so, then slowed to a walk. He already was halted by the time Longarm and the dun reached him. DeCaro leaned down from his saddle and plucked a grass stem that he began to chew.

Longarm was mildly surprised to find that he still had his cheroot jammed between his teeth. He reined the dun around to face toward town. He examined the hillside where the rifle shot surely must have come from, but he could see nothing. No lingering wisp of smoke or any other sign was visible there.

"Do you see where he was?" he asked.

DeCaro shook his head. "Sorry, no."

"Me neither." Frowning, Longarm yanked his Winchester from the boot and stepped down off the dun. "Stay here."

"Where are you going?" DeCaro asked.

"Huntin'," Longarm said with a grunt.

Chapter 33

Longarm shoved the Winchester back into his saddle scabbard, practically growling with disgust as he did so.

"Nothing?" DeCaro asked. While Longarm was prowling along the hillside, he had been joined by two goatherds, their goats grazing nearby under the watchful eyes of their dogs.

"Nothing," Longarm confirmed. "I found the place where he shot from. Found his spent brass, plain old .44-40 like half the men in this country shoot, but of him I didn't find so much as a footprint."

The Mexicans asked something and DeCaro responded at some length. When he was done speaking, the two nodded their understanding of what had happened and spoke some more.

"I already asked them if they saw anything," DeCaro said. "They didn't. Sorry."

"Are these some of the fellas you wanted to run into today?" Longarm asked.

"No, they aren't, but they told me where I can find one of those men anyway."

"Then let's go there."

"Uh, not just yet," DeCaro said.

Longarm lifted an eyebrow.

"It's a matter of hospitality. These fellows will be insulted if we don't at least have a cup of coffee with them." He laughed. "Longarm, by the time this day is over, I'll be surprised if you haven't pissed a dozen times and still have a bladder that full near about to bursting."

Longarm glanced back in the direction that rifle shot had come from, but he said, "Coffee it will be then. But I'm betting these fellas don't make it as good as Nell Tyler does."

DeCaro was right. Longarm felt positively waterlogged by the time they rode back into Dwyer.

Instead of putting the dun back into John Tyler's barn, he left it and his tack at the livery stable and walked back to the jail in the courthouse basement.

He was weary and discouraged after a day of talking with one goatherd after another. They must have spoken with a dozen or more of the Mexican herders, but they'd learned nothing, or anyway close to it.

All of them said they only intended to defend themselves from the Basques, who according to the Mexicans had threatened to kill the goats and the goatherds alike.

While ruffling his dog behind the ears, one fellow from Sonora chuckled and, as translated by Anthony DeCaro, said, "But there is good news. They do not wish to kill our dogs too."

"Yeah. That's real encouraging."

"Yes, but we are ready for them," the Mexican said, hefting a beat-up trapdoor Springfield.

Now Longarm yawned and trudged back to the courthouse. He was tired and faced another long night of standing guard in the jail. The good news there was that he could bolt the door and stretch out on the bunk in the vacant cell.

Just what the rest of Dwyer was doing in the way of law enforcement he had no idea as both he and John Tyler were fully occupied by the needs of the moment.

There would be hell to pay if a shooting war broke out between the Basques and the Mexicans, so that had to be the first priority. Any petty crimes that might be occurring in the town would just have to bide their time until after the crisis was past and Tyler could get back to the probably dull routine of enforcing the laws of Dwyer and of McConnell County.

Longarm was pleased to see there was no group of disgruntled herdsmen, neither Basques nor Mexicans, loitering in the vicinity of the jailhouse steps. He hoped that was a sign that things were cooling off at least a little. If so, he would give himself some of the credit, for closing down both Rosie's and Doris's saloon. Men, even angry men, tend to act much more rationally when they are sober.

He yawned again and started down the steps into the courthouse basement.

He stopped short on the third step.

His Colt slid smoothly out of the leather and into his hand.

The jailhouse door was standing open, and there was no glow of lamplight coming from inside.

Chapter 34

"Damn them. *God damn them!*" Longarm howled. He meant it literally and not merely as a common vulgarity.

Whoever did this, he thought, truly should be damned.

John Tyler, sheriff of McConnell County, Wyoming Territory, lay on the stone floor with a bullet hole in his forehead and the back of his head blown off. Blood and gray brains flooded the floor beneath him. His eyes stared sightlessly toward the ceiling. His sawed-off shotgun lay on the floor half a dozen feet away.

"I told you, dammit," Longarm groaned. "I told you. Don't open the door till I come back. Why, John? Why the hell did you open up? And who was it done this to you?"

He stepped around the corpse, trying not to get any blood on his boots, and looked into the back room where the cells were. If Altameira was gone, he figured, it would be the goatherds who killed John Tyler, and if the man lay dead in his cell it was likely the sheepmen.

Julio Altameira was still locked inside his cell, just as dead as Tyler. He had been shot several times in the upper torso. Longarm did not have to enter the cell to make sure the man was gone from the husk that was his body. The flies that swarmed over his face and fed on his blood were sure enough indication of that.

Scowling, Longarm went back into the outer office. He knelt beside Tyler's body and felt of his throat. He had no expectation of finding vestiges of life there . . . hardly that, after his brains had been blown out of the back of his head . . . but he wanted to check for any remaining warmth in the body.

There was none. Tyler had been dead for some hours, probably since not long after Longarm and Anthony De-Caro rode out in the morning.

Some low-life son of a bitch had come in and murdered both men.

The name of Eli Cruikshank came to mind. Cruikshank had every appearance of a man who not only could use a gun but did so, swiftly and with deadly result.

Longarm tucked his suspicions away for the time being. There were other, more pressing things that had to be taken care of.

He left the sheriff's office and walked over to the barbershop, where Bert was sitting in his own chair with a newspaper opened before him. He looked up when Longarm came in.

"Why, hello, Marshal. Ready for another shave so soon? Or a trim, perhaps? I have a tub in the back where a man can get a bath, but that room has, um, a body in it. Some folks mind that sort of thing."

"That room is fixing to have two more bodies in it," Longarm said. He told the barber/surgeon/undertaker where to find his next projects. "The one of 'em is locked inside a cell. You'll find the keys hanging on the wall in the outer room."

"Sheriff Tyler, you say?"

"I do say. Unfortunately."

"So sad for his pretty little wife. Sad for the whole county for that matter."

"I damn sure agree with that," Longarm said with feeling. "John was a good man. A better man than whoever done this deed."

"I couldn't agree more. Uh, pardon me for asking, but who will be paying for my services?"

"The county, I reckon. Check with them about it."

"Of course. But burials on the county's dime don't come with any extras."

"Take it up with the clerk." Longarm turned and left the barbershop.

He stopped next in the courthouse, mounting the stone steps and going inside to the clerk's office, where he informed Benjamin Laffler of the shooting and asked, "You didn't hear anything this morning? Any gunshots? Anything at all?"

"No, I did not, Marshal, and I think I would have. It is usually quiet in Dwyer and I've had the windows open all day, ever since I got here."

"When d'you get to work, Mr. Laffler?" Longarm asked.

"Eight thirty. Promptly every day at that time."

"All right, thanks." That meant Tyler and the goatherd were very likely shot after Longarm left and before Laffler arrived upstairs, call it eight o'clock give or take a few minutes. "I expect you'll have to hire someone to clean up down there soon as Bert has the bodies removed. And you can expect him to come talk to you about the county payin' for their burying."

Laffler shrugged. "Bert is something of a cheapskate, all the time fretting about money, but he does good enough work." Laffler chuckled. "He hasn't had any complaints from his undertaking customers anyway."

"Yeah, sure." Longarm was not in much of a mood for Laffler's humor or anyone else's. Not considering the chore that remained for him to do.

He left the courthouse and headed up the street toward John Tyler's house, where a lovely young woman did not yet know that she was now a widow.

Lordy, he hated to have to do this sort of thing.

Chapter 35

Word about the murders must have spread through Dwyer faster than a telegraph could have carried it. When Longarm arrived at the Tyler house, there was already a gaggle of church women there, half a dozen of them in the parlor comforting a pale and stricken Nell Tyler while more of the church ladies were in Nell's kitchen preparing tea and whatever.

Longarm figured he would offer his condolences at a better time. He quietly slipped upstairs and gathered his things. It would not be proper for him to stay in the house now that John was dead and Nell would be alone.

He was on his way out—he wasn't sure exactly where he was out to—when one of the church women stopped him. "You are that marshal who was supposed to help John, aren't you?"

"Yes, ma'am," he said, quickly setting his carpetbag down and removing his hat. "I am that."

The woman sniffed loudly and said, "If you had done your job properly, that dear child over there would still have her husband." She was practically aquiver with indignation and looked like she wanted to slap his face.

"Yes, ma'am," he said. "I expect you're right about that." What the hell else could he say? The simple truth was that he agreed with her. He had come here to help. Now Sheriff Tyler was murdered and a helpless prisoner along with him. And Custis Long had done not a damn thing to prevent the murders.

Nell Tyler came up behind the woman, and Longarm figured he would be in for more well-earned condemnation from the young widow. Instead Nell very softly and with steely conviction said, "Find whoever did this, Marshal Long. Find them and kill the sons of bitches. Kill them all."

"Yes, ma'am," he said, not knowing what else he could say under the circumstances. "I'll do all I can."

"Don't bring them to trial, Marshal. Shoot them down like the dogs they are," Nell said.

"Yes, ma'am."

By tomorrow, he figured, Nell would regret her outburst. By then she would surely change her mind about wanting an eye for an eye. In the meantime it did no harm to agree with her.

The woman who'd accused him of failing Tyler put an arm around Nell's shoulders and, with two other ladies helping, led her back into the parlor, where they pressed a teacup into one hand and a cookie into the other.

Longarm tugged his Stetson back into place, picked up his carpetbag, and got the hell out of there. He liked the ladies just fine one at a time, but fluttering, chirping bunches of them tended to make him nervous.

He found the alley behind Helen Birch's saloon, went inside, and put his things in her tiny bedroom. If she did not want them there, well, he could find somewhere else to sleep. In the sheriff's office if necessary, even though the place reeked of the heavy, copper stink of blood.

He went back through the alley and around to the front of the saloon—it wouldn't do Helen's reputation any favors for her patrons to see him coming out of the big woman's private quarters—and reentered from the street.

With both Doris's and Rosie's places shuttered and silent for the time being, Helen was doing a heavy trade. The place was jam-packed with local men and even a few rather nervous-looking whores. Longarm guessed Helen did not approve of them, since she did not normally allow any of the working girls to ply their trade in her place.

He pushed his way through the crowd and got Helen's attention.

"Hello, Marshal. We've heard what happened to Sheriff Tyler and that prisoner you had in there. I'm sorry to hear it. John Tyler was a good man."

"That he was, Helen, thanks." He hesitated for a moment then said, "You ain't gonna like what I have t' tell you now."

"More shootings?" she asked quickly.

"No, nothin' like that, but I'm afraid I got to shut you down too. I don't want folks, any folks, getting liquored up right now. This could turn ugly, and I don't want that. So shut 'er down now, please."

Helen became silent. She spent a moment in thought, probably thinking about defying him. After all, she was doing a great deal of business now that she was the only saloon in town, at least the only open one. She pondered the order and then she nodded. "All right. Under the circumstances that is a reasonable request."

The woman walked to the center of her bar and in a booming voice called out, "That is it, gentlemen. And, um, ladies. We have been ordered to close, so everyone finish your drinks and leave now."

"What if we don't want to do that?" a male voice called out from somewhere in the crowd.

"Then you will be arrested," Longarm responded.

"Just asking," the same voice said, in not nearly so belligerent a tone this time.

The patrons very quickly tossed back whatever drinks they had remaining and made for the door. Within minutes the saloon was empty save for Helen and Longarm.

"I, uh, was kinda hoping you'd take in a boarder for the next few days," Longarm said. "I put my things in the back there."

Helen said nothing. But she locked the front door, turned the CLOSED sign, and pulled the blinds.

Then she smiled. "Would you like a drink, Custis?"

"Yes. And more'n that afterward." He reached for her and she came into his arms.

Neither one of them remembered the promised drink.

Chapter 36

Longarm took her standing up, bent over the whiskey-stained bar in her saloon. He took her without kissing or foreplay, just lifting her dress and shoving his suddenly insistent cock into her from behind.

Helen seemed to understand his urgency. Longarm did not really understand it himself.

Death could do that, he supposed. Fucking was an affirmation of life, and he was indeed alive, while others, for whatever reason and by whatever hand, were cold and dead.

He drove into Helen as hard and as deep as he could. She shuddered and trembled and within a dozen thrusts began to respond, her pussy clenching around him as she built to one climax after another long before Longarm's explosive gush of cum.

He came in a great outpouring of hot fluids, then his knees went weak and he fell forward onto the woman, giving his weight to Helen to carry.

Longarm stayed like that for long moments, leaning on her as she bent over the bar, until his strength returned and he pushed himself upright.

Once Longarm had withdrawn, the hem of Helen's dress fell and she straightened upright.

She turned and peered into his eyes without comment for what must have been the better part of a full minute. Then she reached up and gently touched his face. She leaned forward and kissed him lightly, gently.

She smiled. "You needed that."

Longarm nodded. "Aye, I did. I dunno why exactly, but . . . yeah. I did."

Her smile became wider and she kissed him again. "I'm glad I was here for you."

Longarm hugged her. "You're a good woman, Helen Birch. A damned good woman."

"Why, thank you, sir," she said with another smile. "Now help yourself to a drink while I go make us some supper."

"Come t' think of it, I'm close on to starvation," Longarm said, returning the lady's smile. "Then later on we can go in t' that bed o' yours and get naked, do things nice and proper."

She laughed. "I didn't know there was a 'proper' way to do that particular thing."

"You didn't?" he said, pretending her comment shocked him. "Reckon in that case I'll have t' show you how."

"After we eat." She leaned forward and kissed him. "Now, help yourself to that drink. I'll go make our supper."

Chapter 37

"That was fine," he lied, pushing his plate away. Helen's supper had not been particularly tasty, but it filled the emptiness in his belly.

"Do you want to, um . . . ?" She seemed suddenly shy.

"Yes, I do, but not now," he told her. "I got to make the rounds of town. See to it that things are quiet. I'll come back after I see to things, but I got to do that first."

"All right. Whatever you need to do," she said.

Longarm stood and stretched. He reached for his hat and put on the coat he had shed before eating. "Do you have a lantern I could borrow? A bull's-eye if you have one o' those."

"I have a regular lantern. Will that do?"

"Sure."

"Wait here." Helen went into the saloon and returned moments later carrying a rather battered lantern. She filled it from a can of coal oil, lifted the globe, and lighted it for him.

"Thanks." He kissed her and went out the back door carrying the lantern low with his left hand.

He went first to the courthouse and around back to the sheriff's office. The door still gaped slightly open, and no one had yet come to start cleaning up the mess inside. A thief could have a fine time in there, stealing the county's shotguns and rifles. There was nothing he could do about the door, but he did go in—carefully because of all the blood and gore that remained on the floor—and moved the valuable firearms into a cell, which he locked, putting the key into his pocket.

From the courthouse he walked over to the Tyler house and around back to the little barn. There he fed and watered DeCaro's dun horse and Tyler's mare as well. He doubted anyone would think about the horses. The house showed lights from the windows, and there was still a crowd of ladies inside trying to comfort Nell. He could see them through the open windows and hear snippets of conversation. John Tyler's death seemed to have turned into a social function for the churches in Dwyer.

It had been a long time since Longarm had served as a town lawman, but he remembered how. He went downtown and walked the business district, checking to see that doors were locked and that no one was lurking in the alleys.

He passed through the alleys as well, Helen's lantern showing the way.

As he came out of a narrow opening between Sam Johnson's mercantile and a leather-working shop, he almost bumped into Eli Cruikshank.

Longarm was keyed up and came close to drawing down on the lanky Texan.

"Whoa," Cruikshank said, throwing his hands up and taking a step back. "I didn't mean to startle you, Marshal. I'm sorry."

"Yeah, I, uh, I guess I'm a mite touchy tonight," Longarm confessed.

"It's no wonder, the sheriff being murdered and all," Cruikshank said. "That's why I was looking for you, actually."

"You know something about it?"

Cruikshank lowered his hands and said, "Not really. Which is what I want you to know. The Mexican was murdered right along with the sheriff the way I heard it. Is that right?"

Longarm nodded.

"So the first thing you would've had in mind, I'm sure, is that I did it," Cruikshank said. "That one stands to reason. I would think so too in your place, but what I want you to know is that I didn't do it. I'll kill a man, sure, but I'll keep it within the law and I'll own up to it afterward. And I did not kill Sheriff Tyler nor that Mexican."

"Where were you early this morning, Eli?" Longarm asked.

"In camp with the Basques and their flocks. About a half mile up from where we were when you were out there."

"You have witnesses who will confirm what you say?"

Cruikshank nodded. "I do, Marshal." Then he smiled a little and shrugged. "Of course they'd lie for me about that. Which you likely know already."

"Puts me in an awkward spot, don't it," Longarm said.

"Yeah. I guess it does," Cruikshank agreed. "So are you going to take me in?" He grinned and added, "Or try to?"

"If I have reason to take you in, Eli, why, I reckon I will do that. The thing is, at the moment I don't have any proof that you are the one responsible for those murders."

"Don't have and you won't have, Marshal, for I didn't do them," Cruikshank said.

"I hope you're telling me the truth, Eli. Assuming that you are innocent, do you have any idea who might've done them?"

The Texas gunman shook his head. "I'd help you if I

could, but I don't have no idea about it. The news reached the Basque camp about midday, which is the first I heard of it. I know it was none of our bunch though. I can give you my word on that."

"You trust all of those fellas?" Longarm asked.

Cruikshank grinned again. "Not really, but I know them well enough by now to be sure that if any of them *did* do those shootings, they would've bragged about it around the fire afterward. There was a lot of talk about the Mexican today, but it was all about what they *wanted* to do to him, nothing about what they *had* done to him. If you see the difference."

"I hope that's straight talk, Eli."

"You have my word on it, Marshal."

"That's good enough, Eli. For now." Longarm turned and walked on, making his rounds of the sleepy town of Dwyer.

Chapter 38

Sleepy, hell!

Longarm had not gone half a block before a flash of gunpowder flared behind him. A bullet sizzled past his left ear and hit the siding of Bert's barbershop with a solid thump.

At almost the same instant Longarm spun, crouching, his Colt in his hand.

He could see . . . not a damn thing.

The street was dark and silent. Longarm thought he heard distant footsteps, but he was not sure about that, and his night vision was poor thanks to the bright light of the lantern he was carrying.

He quickly backed into the doorway of the barbershop, lifted the lantern bail, and blew out the flame. The sudden darkness blinded him all the further.

"Son of a *bitch*," he mumbled.

The shooter had to know exactly where he was, but Longarm had no clue as to where the shooter had been. And might still be.

That was the problem. The cocksucker might still be

there—somewhere—waiting for Longarm to make a target of himself again. The receding footsteps he thought he'd heard might well have been an illusion or they could have been the sound of someone quite sensibly running the hell away from trouble.

Longarm blinked rapidly, trying to force his night vision to return. The effort did nothing of the kind. It did not help a thing. Probably did not hurt either, but that was no consolation. He needed to be able to see. *Right damned now!*

The .45 in his hand felt solid and reassuring.

But he needed some-damned-where to point it.

Longarm felt suddenly vulnerable and exposed.

The shooter had probably gone. Probably took his shot and then ran.

But the important part there was that word "probably." The son of a bitch could still be there. Somewhere.

Longarm's back had been turned at the moment of the gunshot. He was aware of the flash and the general direction but not the exact spot where the shot came from, and his lantern-ruined night vision did nothing to help.

After several long moments he stood upright, his knee joints cracking. He shoved the Colt back into its leather and took a tentative step out of the shallow niche of Bert's doorway.

No one shot at him. Nothing moved except for a cat that ran streaking from an alley mouth across the street in the direction of the courthouse.

Longarm idly hoped the animal was not on its way down to the courthouse basement to feast on John Tyler's spilled brains.

Just in case it or others like it had that in mind, Longarm crossed over to the courthouse and went to the back. He relighted the lantern and took advantage of the match to light a cheroot too, then went inside the sheriff's office.

He set the lantern on Tyler's desk and rummaged in the drawers until he found a little twine. He went outside, pulled the broken door to, and used the twine to secure it closed. The closure would not keep any humans out if they wanted to come see what they could pilfer, but it should keep cats and dogs and rats away. He hoped. The idea of stray animals making a meal off the mess on the sheriff's office floor was unpleasant. Longarm's stomach roiled at the thought, and he sucked hard on his cigar to get a sour taste out of his mouth.

He finished making a circuit of Dwyer's businesses without seeing another soul.

And without being shot at.

Chapter 39

"Are you all right?" Helen asked. She was seated at her kitchen table. "If you don't mind me saying so, Custis, you look like hell warmed over."

"That's reasonable," he told her, "'cause that's just about how I feel right now."

"What happened out there?"

"Someone shot at me" was all the explanation he gave. The real problem was the image he had in his mind now about rats eating parts of John Tyler. He did not tell Helen about that, though.

"Would you like a drink?" she offered.

Longarm smiled. "I would, but all the saloons in town been shut down by some officious son of a bitch."

"True," she said, "but I have a secret stash of rye whiskey. How's about a shot and a beer?"

"Will you join me?" he asked.

Helen laughed. "I don't drink."

"You're in the business, but . . ."

"I would have some coffee with you," she said. She took

a lamp down off the wall and carried it into the bar, Longarm following at her heels.

"Sit down, dear. I'll bring you something."

Longarm chose a seat at one of the small tables and idly riffled through a deck of cards he found there, laying out a hand of solitaire. Helen served him the promised shot and brew, then disappeared for a few minutes. When she returned she was carrying a cup of coffee and a plate of cookies.

"Here," she said. "Just what you need." She leaned down to kiss him. That kiss led to more. And more led to something much more.

The big woman smiled. "Could we do it in the bed this time, dear? That bar is hard. And cold."

He kissed her. "Sorry."

"Oh, you needn't apologize. I know you needed me, and it pleases me very much that I was able to be there when you did."

"It occurs to me, madam, that you are a very nice woman." He smiled. "As well as being one damned fine fuck."

"Why, thank you, sir," she said with a curtsy.

Longarm laughed and bowed low, then offered his elbow. Acting quite the gentleman, he escorted the lady into her bedroom and watched with pleasure as she took her clothes off. Only when Helen was naked did Longarm strip.

She peered at his erection for a moment. Reached out and touched it. Then, quite ladylike, said, "Now, sir, if you will oblige me," she looked at him and laughed, "I will fuck your brains out."

The reference to brains was not something he really wanted to hear just then.

But Helen dropped to her knees and took him into her mouth.

Longarm completely forgot about anything beyond the moment.

Chapter 40

Longarm woke well before dawn, Helen snug against his side. He eased slowly out of the bed, careful to not disturb her. Last night, between bouts of vigorous lovemaking, she had mentioned that she had not had a day off in years, so his forced closing of the saloons in town had served to give her a vacation, and she intended to make the most of it by sleeping in.

He picked up his clothing and carried it into the kitchen, where he washed with the still slightly warm water in the oven reservoir. He could find nothing more substantial than a handful of bar rags to dry off with, but they served the purpose well enough.

Once dressed, he left through the alley, emerging onto the streets of Dwyer in the soft light of the coming dawn. It was chilly and Longarm shivered, then headed for the only light he could see in the business district.

The shade was up at the café window and he could see someone working in there. It was not the usual fellow, but then patrons would be coming by to eat both early and late. It only made sense for several people to work in shifts.

Longarm tapped on the glass to get the man's attention.

The fellow came to the door and through the glass said, "What do you want?"

"In," Longarm told him. "I'm hungry."

"I'm not open yet."

"Trust me," Longarm told him. "Yes, you are." He reached for his wallet to display his badge, but the man said, "I know who you are."

"Then let me in, will you? Please?"

"Oh, all right, but I got work to do here. I got biscuits to bake." He turned the lock and slid a bolt back, then opened the door for Longarm to enter.

"You got coffee?"

"Does a dog have ticks? Of course I got coffee."

"Coffee and some of your biscuits would be good enough for me," Longarm said.

"All right then, but sit at the counter. I don't have time to be running back and forth to a table."

"That's fine with me. By the way, I'm Long." He stuck his hand out to shake.

The café man laughed, then shook.

"Did I say something funny?" Longarm asked.

Shoulders heaving up and down from barely contained laughter the café man managed to say, "Yeah. You did."

Longarm's eyebrows went up.

"You're Long. I'm Short. Johnny Short."

Longarm grinned. "I see what you mean. Pleasure t' meet you, Johnny."

"Likewise. Sit over there and I'll bring you that coffee." Still chuckling, he added, "Maybe I can find something more than just coffee and biscuits for you too. Ham, maybe a few eggs?"

"Sounds perfect." Longarm was smiling when he sat down at the counter.

Twenty minutes later, with most of a fine breakfast warming Longarm's belly from the inside out, a tiny bell over the door tinkled and two men dressed for hard travel came in. They chose seats at the counter one stool down from Longarm.

"Good morning. You gents are up early," he said.

"Yeah, dammit. We expected to get here yesterday. Wired the customer that we would be. But we busted a wheel. Ran over a damn rock and busted it clean. Then we had a bitch of a time trying to get the wagon jacked up so we could get that one off and a new one on. Haven't had a chance to get hardly any sleep as we're already late on this delivery."

"You're freighters?" Longarm asked.

"Yep. We're making a special haul up from Cheyenne. Rush order and heavy as hell." He looked around as if he could visualize the grasslands of McConnell County through the walls of the little café. "Damned if I understand why, though. I mean, what's so special about the hunting up here that anyone would want all this shit?"

"What shit do you mean?" Longarm asked, taking a swallow of coffee.

"Cartridges," the freighter said. "Cases of .45-60 cartridges and shotgun shells, and those sons of bitches weigh a ton. We got a whole wagonload of them. And now we get here and the consignee isn't open. What can we do? We left the wagon at the loading dock and walked our mules over to the livery. Now we're hungry as bears and about as ornery."

"Can't say as I blame you," Longarm said. He leaned forward and looked at the other of the two, most likely the swamper, while the talkative gent would be the driver. That other one had not said a word. He was certainly interested in the coffee Johnny Short set in front of him though.

"Can we have another of those?" the driver asked, motioning toward Longarm's plate.

"Coming right up," Johnny told him.

The driver sighed, leaned back a little, stretched with his arms over his head. He looked back at Longarm and said, "You would think somebody was fixing to go to war up here with all that ammunition on hand."

"Yeah," Longarm mused. "Wouldn't you." He quickly finished his breakfast and dropped a quarter on the counter, casting a wary eye and wondering who they were selling all that ammo to. "Thanks, Johnny." To the freighters he said, "Take it easy, fellas. I hope the rest o' your day goes better for you."

Chapter 41

On his way out Longarm met the barber, Bert, who was just coming into the café.

"Good morning, Johnny," Bert said, taking his cap off and draping it onto a peg on the coat rack by the door. "And good morning to you, Marshal."

"Mornin'," Longarm agreed. "Have you finished with the bodies yet?" There was no need to specify exactly which bodies he meant. There would not be so very many of them at any one time in a town the size of Dwyer. At least he hoped there would not be a surplus of them anytime in the near future.

"Oh, yes." Bert sat at a table and motioned to the chair opposite his. "Join me?"

"I just finished my breakfast," Longarm said.

"Then have some coffee with me. I hate to eat alone."

"All right." He turned back toward the counter and said, "Johnny, I have a change o' plans here, so don't toss my coffee cup into the dish pail just yet."

"You want a refill I take it?"

"I do indeed. But only 'cause you make such good coffee," he said with a smile.

"Hell, for that this refill will be free."

Longarm laughed. "All your refills are free."

"Yes, and this one is too."

"And I'll have my usual," Bert said, using his foot to push a chair away from the table for Longarm.

Longarm noticed that a flood of soft light coming in through the windows showed that it was coming dawn. Out on the street people were beginning to stir, starting their daily routines. More townspeople began to drift into the café.

Johnny brought two cups of coffee and a bowl of porridge for Bert, along with a can of condensed milk and a bowl of sugar. The morning cook went back behind the counter and removed another pan of biscuits from the oven, shoved a fresh pan in to bake, and started cracking eggs into a huge frying pan. His day was well under way now.

"Anything unusual about those bodies?" Longarm asked.

"Sure. They're dead."

"I meant . . ."

"I know what you meant, Marshal. I was just funning a little. If it matters to you, I'd say they were both shot with the same gun. It was a pistol and somewhat unusual in this day and age. They were shot with round ball, not modern cartridge."

"Round shot could be from a shotgun," Longarm said.

Bert nodded. "You'd think so. Double-ought is about the same size as a .36 Navy. But these had to come from a cap-and-ball revolver. Anything fired from a shotgun would've done even more damage than what there was."

"Jesus," Longarm said, shuddering at the memory of what John Tyler's corpse had looked like. "You mean it could've got worse?"

"Believe me. It would have been even worse from a shotgun. There wouldn't have been much of anything left of the back of Tyler's skull. And the Mexican . . . what was his name?"

"Altameira. Julio Altameira."

"You'll have to write that down for me so I can put it on his marker. Anyway, this Altameira was locked in his cell. The shooter couldn't have been more than eight feet from him. He was hit four times, the shots spaced fairly close together but not like they would have been from a shotgun. A shotgun fired that close up would have hit almost like solid shot. Damn near like a cannonball. I recovered all the bullets from the body and went back later to look inside the cell. Looked on the wall for bullet strikes. On the floor to make sure none were lost there. There were only the four balls, and they all found their mark."

Longarm nodded. "And a shotgun would've left . . . what does a twelve-gauge shell carry? Nine balls that size, isn't it?"

"Right. And there were only four. So the weapon had to be a pistol."

"Bert, you would make one hell of a fine detective, d'you know that?"

The barber beamed at the compliment.

"More coffee, gentlemen?" Johnny asked on his rounds among the now busy tables. He was carrying the pot with him and filling cups and taking orders as he went.

"Not for me, thanks," Longarm said, "and I'd best get out o' here to make room for your customers." He laughed. "I don't think just everybody likes to set with the law so early in the morning." To Bert he said, "Thanks for that information. It could be important."

"If there is anything I can do . . ."

"I'll ask. And thank you for that too."

He tipped his hat toward Johnny Short, who by then was on the far side of the room, and again to Bert, then headed out to see what he could see.

What he wanted to see was an answer to the murder of Sheriff John Tyler and Julio Altameira.

Chapter 42

"Oh, shit," Longarm mumbled under his breath. It was barely dawn and the Mexicans were gathering in front of the courthouse. They looked like it would take little provocation to turn them into a mob. All of them were armed. There seemed to be an awful lot of them. Apparently they had turned their goats over to the protective care of their herding dogs while all the humans headed for town to seek redress for the murder of Julio Altameira.

Longarm grabbed the attention of a pair of boys on their way to school—at least they were carrying book bags—and motioned them to him.

"How'd you fellows like to earn a dime apiece?"

The taller and presumably older of the two eyed him with suspicion, while the little guy, nine or ten years old, lit up with eagerness.

"What do we got to do, Marshal?" the young one asked.

"I want you to run over to the livery and tell Mr. DeCaro that I need him here in front of the courthouse." He reached into his pocket and brought out some change, looked at it and announced, "I don't have two dimes, so how's about I give the two o' you a quarter. You can figure out how to split it later. But first you go get Mr. DeCaro."

Now it was the older boy who looked happy about the deal. Longarm suspected he would give his brother the short end of the stick when they got change for their quarter.

"That's a deal, Marshal," the older one said.

Longarm handed over the quarter, and the two boys raced away in the direction of the livery.

He started toward the Mexicans, only to be brought up short by the sight of fifteen or twenty Basques coming down the street, Eli Cruikshank leading the way. They too were armed. Much better armed than the Mexicans in fact. Their rifles were far more modern than the outmoded shotguns and single-shot weapons of the Mexicans.

Longarm changed direction and met the Basques head-on.

"I don't need this shit today, Eli. Turn your boys around and head 'em back to the sheep camps."

"We've been accused . . ."

"You've been accused of nothing," Longarm said sharply. "Not a damn thing. I'm in the middle of investigating what happened, and at least at this point it don't have anything to do with you or your Basques. If I find out different, you'll be one of the first to know. In the meantime I want you to take your people right back out of town. I got troubles enough without you putting your oar in the water."

Cruikshank turned and spoke to the Basques, several of whom responded with gestures that spoke clearly enough that they did not like what Eli was telling them. Longarm did not need to know their language to understand that much.

The Basques glared at Longarm. He glared right back at them. Be damned if he was going to be intimidated by them. He was the law here and they would by damn abide by what he said.

Eli spoke to them again, and they seemed to relax at

least a little bit. Then Eli turned to Longarm and said, "I told them they have to go back to camp but that you'll be sending those cocksuckers," he inclined his head toward the Mexicans milling around in front of the courthouse, "back to their camps too." Cruikshank's eyes narrowed slightly when he said, "Isn't that right, Marshal?"

"It's right," Longarm said. "I'll be dispersing them quick as I get DeCaro here so's I got somebody to translate for me."

"I speak Spanish," Eli said.

Longarm grinned. "I'll bet you do, neighbor, but damned if I'm gonna trust you to do my talking. No offense, mind you."

"None taken."

"Good. Now turn your boys around and get them well outa town before I send the Mexicans packing in that same direction. I wouldn't want you all to bump into each other on your way home."

Cruikshank paused for a moment, then turned and spoke to the Basques. Somewhat reluctantly—but obediently, that was the important thing—they complied with the order to disperse.

Longarm breathed a little easier once it was the backsides of the Basques that he was seeing going down the street.

The Basques had barely cleared the block when Anthony DeCaro came hustling down the street looking like he was not yet fully awake.

"Sorry to take so long, Longarm. I had a mare go colicky last night and spent most of the night walking her."

"Did she make it?"

"I think so. Might be a little soon to tell."

While they spoke, they walked in the direction of the crowd of goatherds. Taking up a position between the Mexicans and the front of the courthouse steps, Longarm said, "Tell them their presence here ain't necessary. Tell them

I'm lookin' for whoever it was that gunned down their friend Altameira. Tell them that person will face the full weight of the law when I do catch up with him. Which I will for damn certain sure. Tell them to go back to their camps and leave me to get on with what I got to do. Tell them it only makes things harder if I got to be worrying about them when I oughta be going about getting my work done."

Anthony gave the group a longish spiel in Spanish. Longer, Longarm thought, than a simple translation would have required, but that was all right. Just so it got the message across.

Several of the goatherds had questions. DeCaro was able to answer most of them, but once he turned to Longarm and said, "They want to know if Julio will receive Yankee justice even though he was nothing but a greaser to you . . . to us, I should say . . . to us gringos."

"Tell them I guaran-damn-tee it," Longarm said.

Anthony spoke some more, and slowly the anger on the faces of the Mexicans seemed to recede. They held their shotguns lower, letting the weapons dangle from one hand instead of carrying them high with both hands. That was a good sign, Longarm thought.

"They'll go," Anthony said, "but they have some shopping to do in town, so they won't be leaving just yet. If, uh, if that is all right with you."

"Sure. Just so's they don't cause no trouble. Fact is, it's probably a good thing to let the Basques get well clear of town before these boys head out."

Anthony relayed that message in Spanish, and the Mexicans began moving as a body toward the businesses along the main street of Dwyer.

Longarm watched them on their way, the opposite direction from the Basques, then he walked around to the back of the courthouse.

Chapter 43

The very messy aftermath of the murders was still there,
dark red and lumpy, on the sheriff's office floor. Longarm
was pissed off. He hustled back outside and around to the
front of the handsome courthouse building, then stormed up
the steps and inside.

County clerk Benjamin Laffler physically recoiled when
Longarm charged toward him, eyes as cold as a rattle-
snake's. "What . . . ?"

"Don't give me no 'what' bullshit," Longarm snapped.
"You know damn good and well what has me riled."

"It is early in the morning and . . ."

"I don't care if it's the middle of the damn night. Now
you either get a clean-up crew down there in that office to
put things right or you'll grab a mop and go down to do it
yourself, I don't much care which. But right now I'm gonna
make the rounds around this town. When I get done with
that, that office *better* be suitable for folks to come in and
out of. Do you understand me, Laffler? Do you?"

Without waiting for an answer, Longarm spun on his
heels and left the clerk's office, still fuming to the point it

was a wonder there wasn't steam coming out of his ears.

He walked around to a side street and down it for a few paces, to the mouth of the alley that led to the back of Helen Birch's saloon.

There was no sign of the Mexicans, who seemed to have disappeared off the streets of Dwyer, and the Basques were well on their way back to their sheep camps.

Trouble seemed to have been averted.

For now.

He let himself into the back of Helen's place and tiptoed into the kitchen, where as quietly as he could he added some chunks of coal to the stove and moved the coffeepot to the front to heat.

"Good morning."

He turned to see Helen standing in the doorway to her tiny bedroom. Her hair was tousled, her face was blotchy with patches of red where she had been lying on a pillow, and she was bare-ass naked.

Longarm smiled. "Damn, you look good this morning."

"Liar," she said.

"Want me t' prove it?" he challenged.

"All right, tough guy. See if you can prove it."

Longarm crossed the room to stand in front of her. He took Helen into his arms and kissed her, long and deeply. She had morning breath and must have been eating garlic not too long ago. And he thought she tasted just fine.

He bent, put an arm behind her knees, and picked her up—no small task with a woman Helen's size—then carried her right back into the bedroom she had just emerged from and plopped her down onto the bed.

Without comment he stripped his clothes off, his erection standing tall even before he got his pants off, and lay on top of her.

Helen opened herself to him, thrusting upward with her

hips to meet Longarm's downward strokes, taking him deep and giving him the warmth and comfort of her body.

Soon her breathing quickened and she began to whimper with her own pleasure, while giving even better than she got.

Longarm came in an explosion of sensation. Helen reached her own climax seconds after him. Her arms tightened around him and she gasped for breath.

He lifted his head so that he could look into her face. "Well?" he demanded.

Helen smiled. She whispered, "You proved it, tough guy."

"The coffee should be hot by now," he responded.

Helen laughed and pushed him off of her. "Let's start the day, shall we?"

"Hell, I thought we just did," Longarm told her.

Chapter 44

Longarm made a circuit around the businesses of Dwyer, then walked back to the courthouse, intending to inspect the sheriff's office and primed to rip Benjamin Laffler a fresh asshole if there was not at least a cleaning crew hard at work in the basement. He was stopped in mid-grumble by a gent wearing sleeve garters and an eyeshade.

"Might I have a word with you, Marshal?"

"Sure thing," Longarm said. "I don't mind talkin'."

"My name is Jensen Dibble. I am one of the county supervisors of McConnell County." He made the announcement but did not offer a hand to shake.

"Reckon you know who I am," Longarm said. "What is it that's got your stomach acids rumbling, Mr. Dibble?"

"You already know that the well-being of our county and this town are very much the same thing." He said that as if he expected Longarm to deny knowing any such thing.

"Uh-huh." Longarm reached inside his coat, brought out a cheroot, and lighted it. He was running low on the slender cigars. Perhaps Sam Johnson had some in his store. If not, well, another cigar would do. If he really had to, he could make do with cut tobacco and some cigarette papers.

"The sheep- and goatherders represent a major portion of the trade conducted in Dwyer, Marshal, and the businesses they conduct that trade with represent our tax base. In short, both the town and the county depend on the business those people bring in."

"Thank you for givin' me that lesson in local doin's, Mr. Dibble, but what the fuck does it have to do with anything?"

"You closed down the saloons," Dibble said, his tone of voice suggesting it was an accusation.

"Yeah, I did that all right."

"Without prior authorization, I might add."

Longarm snorted. "If I'd asked permission, them saloons would still be open, and both the Basques and the Mexicans would be getting drunk about now. Drunk leads to trouble, mister. Drunk leads to shooting. I don't want no shooting. I'm tryin' to *stop* a war, not pile fuel on the fire."

Dibble ignored Longarm's comments. "You've run those Basque gentlemen out of town."

"Uh-huh. I damn sure did that too." The smoke from Longarm's cigar found its way into Dibble's face. Dibble angrily waved it away, and Longarm said, "Sorry 'bout that," his tone making it very clear that he was not in the least bit sorry. He exhaled again and more cigar smoke headed Dibble's way.

"We . . . that is the county supervisors and the town council . . . we want you to allow the saloons to reopen. We want you to encourage those people to spend time in the town, not quarantined out in their sheep camps somewhere."

Longarm smiled broadly and said, "Why, Mr. Dibble, I think that is a splendid notion, and I'll take it up with the county sheriff quick as I can."

Dibble scowled. "You know as well as I do that the sheriff has been murdered. That means you seem to be our acting sheriff."

"Why yes, I expect that it does at that," Longarm said, as if the idea had not occurred to him before that moment. "Tell you what then. If you got a complaint about me, you can take it up with U.S. marshal William Vail down in Denver. You want for me to give you his address so's you can reach him there? I'm sure he'd be glad for an excuse to chew my ass. Might even decide to recall me. Fetch me back down there to tell me what a poor job I been doing up here. Meantime you all can pick yourselves a new sheriff to protect this town when the shootin' starts. Which I figure it likely will after one good afternoon and early evening with them saloons open for business."

"We don't . . . that is, I wouldn't think . . ."

"Thanks for tellin' me all this shit, Dibble. Now if you will excuse me . . ." Longarm turned and headed for the back of the courthouse to see how the cleaning crew—if any—was coming along with getting the blood and brains removed.

Chapter 45

The sheriff's office was empty. And clean. Someone had come in and cleared away all the blood and gore left by the murders. They'd even sprinkled something around—vinegar? possibly—to take away the stink of the congealed blood. If there was anything Longarm hated to smell it was blood.

Nothing had been done yet about the door. It would probably have to be replaced so a proper lock could be installed. For the time being then, he thought, it would be best to leave the firearms and any sensitive papers locked in the cell in back. Not that he knew what papers might be sensitive. Nor for that matter did he have any idea what papers, if any, John Tyler might have left here. And he had no inclination to spend the day inside here going over paperwork. He really felt like he could put a stop to the problems between the Basques and the Mexicans, but not if he was sitting in here behind a desk.

Cheroots. Shit, he was past running low. The lone soldier he pulled out of his pocket was his last cigar. With a sigh, he nipped the twist off the end and spat it out, then rolled the cheroot around in his mouth a few times to moisten it.

He found a kitchen match in his side pocket—he was running low on those too—and struck it, then allowed the sulfur to burn off before applying the flame to tobacco and lighted his smoke. "Damn, but that tastes fine," he mumbled to himself.

Probably, he thought, he should walk over to Sam Johnson's mercantile and see what the man carried in the way of cigars.

It would be too much to hope for that the store would carry his particular brand of cheroot, but when it came to his smokes Longarm was not all that particular. Pretty much any decent—emphasis on "decent"—cigar would do, although he really did prefer a good-quality cheroot to the ordinary blunts and panatelas. But hell, he would even smoke a cheap and dirty molasses crook if he had to.

Sighing again, Longarm stood and stretched for a moment, felt of his waist to make sure his Colt was in the precise place where he liked it, then left the sheriff's office.

He did his best to prop the broken door closed behind him, although there was less likelihood that rats and other vermin would be attracted to the place now that there was no blood inside for them to feed on.

Johnson's store was only a short distance around to the other side of the courthouse, across the street and down a little way.

Longarm encountered half a dozen folks on their way about town. Most of them nodded pleasantly enough. A pair of women—he thought he recognized one of them as having comforted Nell Tyler in her time of pain—changed direction so they could confront him.

At first he assumed they were going to ream him out about something. That was common enough with "proper" ladies in his past experience. Instead they were all smiles.

"We can't thank you enough, Marshal," one of them chirped.

"Ma'am?" He blinked, barely stopping himself from taking a step back in anticipation of their anger about one thing or another. He snatched his Stetson off and held it to his belly, more or less hiding the big revolver on his belt.

The nearer, and prettier, of the two smiled broadly. "For closing those horrid saloons. Why, you have almost succeeded in making Dwyer a dry community. I hope now you will speak with Mr. Johnson about the liquor he sells out of his back door."

"I, uh, I didn't know Mr. Johnson does that."

"Oh, yes. Mr. Johnson is a heathen."

"Really, ma'am?"

"Indeed, yes. On Sunday mornings our town council has ordered there be no sales of hard spirits until noon. The saloons, bad as they are, have always cooperated with that law. Mr. Johnson, though, sells raw spirits despite the ordinance. Everyone knows that."

Longarm smiled. "An' now I know it too. Thank you, ladies, for pointin' it out to me."

Not that he had any intention of actually doing anything about it. But it was good to keep the town's womenfolk as happy as he could. And he had not actually made any promises. Just thanked them for the information.

He made a little bow in their direction—that one really wasn't such a bad-looking dame—and went on his way. He was smiling as he did so.

He stepped inside Johnson's store and looked around, but there was no one behind the counter. He did spot a box of reasonably good cheroots beneath the counter's glass top. He was tempted to help himself and leave the payment for what he took, but a dip into his pockets showed that he was completely out of small change. He had not a single coin in his kick. He did have some folding money, but he was damned if he was going to pay a dollar for a two-for-a-nickel cheroot.

Instead he went behind the counter and cracked open the door that led into the storeroom, expecting to find Johnson back there.

He heard someone talking. In Spanish. It definitely was not Sam Johnson's voice.

Scowling, Longarm pushed the door the rest of the way open, worried that one of the disgruntled Mexicans was robbing Johnson. Or worse.

What he found was worse. But not in the way he'd expected.

Chapter 46

What he found was Samuel Johnson alive and well and busily making sales out of a pair of crates that contained brand-new Marlin lever-action rifles. A line of Mexican goatherds waited patiently for Johnson to exchange their gold for his rifles.

Even with that first glimpse, Longarm could see that each goatherd had a pair of gold double eagles in hand. And one fellow held a wad of crumpled paper money.

Two double eagles. Forty dollars. For a twenty-seven-dollar rifle.

In addition to the Marlins, Johnson was selling .45-60 cartridges out of cases of them stacked against the wall.

So this was the freight those boys had been in such a rush to deliver. He'd had his suspicions but now they were confirmed.

Samuel Johnson was arming the Mexicans for a high-powered shooting war.

And the man was making one hell of a profit doing it.

This, Longarm figured, was exactly what people meant when they said "war profiteer."

Almost as bad as what Johnson was egging on here was that there was not a single damned thing that was illegal about it. If men's lives were put at risk in a shooting war between the Basques and the Mexicans, there was no part of it that could come back on Sam Johnson.

If Johnson could find a way to double his profits by putting others at risk, that was entirely legal. All he was doing, he would argue, was selling legal goods to legal buyers, never mind the obscene profits he was pulling in from those transactions.

The Mexicans looked startled as all hell when Longarm walked in on them. They looked like they felt guilty about what they were doing.

Longarm approached Johnson and his open crates of rifles.

A goatherd who was struggling under the weight of a full crate of .45-60 cartridges gave Longarm a nervous look, set his cartridges down on the floor, and scampered out of the storeroom by way of a back door into an alley.

This, then, was where all the Mexicans had disappeared to when they vacated the street near the courthouse.

Others nervously eyed the tall marshal, then they too turned tail and left, most of them without their brand-new Marlins.

"You have no right to be here," Johnson said indignantly.

Longarm nodded. "You're right. I don't. But I'll tell you what I do have the right to do, Sam. I have the right to tell every swingin' dick in the town o' Dwyer an' the county of McConnell what you been doing here. Did you arm the Basques too, Sam? Or just the Meskins?"

"That is none of your damned business."

"Oh, I dunno. I'll have to look into it. Maybe I can charge you with inciting to riot or some shit like that. Between me and my people down in Denver, I'm sure we can poke around and find some charge that will put you behind bars, Sam. Might not be a real long sentence. Ten years or so would be my guess." He smiled. "You can handle that, can't you? Now, if you'll excuse me, I got t' go make a whole lot o' announcements around town. The barbershop, the café, the saloons when I get them open again." He chuckled. "Just think what the good people o' Dwyer are gonna think about their neighbor Sam."

Longarm turned to leave then stopped and turned back again. "And those murders, Sam. I'm gonna look real hard and see can I find some way to connect you with those, for I suspect now that you're the lad as killed John Tyler and Julio Altameira. Think about it. Tyler wouldn't have opened that door to anybody from either the Basque or the Mexican camps. But he'd have opened up to let his good neighbor in. Wouldn't he, Sam?"

"You can't prove shit, lawman," Johnson snarled.

"Damn, Sam. Your happy-face mask is slipping. You're showing your real self now." Longarm wagged a finger in the storekeeper's direction. "You'd best be careful about that if you wanta keep doing business in this town."

Johnson looked like he was ready to explode.

Longarm headed for the door into the store.

He heard the metallic click-clack of a cartridge being jacked into the chamber of a rifle.

Longarm threw himself sideways.

Behind him there was the contained explosion from one of those .45-60 cartridges. The storeroom was filled with noise and billowing white gunsmoke. Splinters flew from the door frame, and Johnson's slug went singing out into the mercantile.

Longarm dropped to a knee trying to get beneath the smoke.

He saw Johnson's legs and triggered a .45 slug into the man's left knee.

Johnson screamed, and racked the lever on the Marlin he had snatched up and fired again. The storekeeper dropped to the floor, his left leg no longer able to hold him upright.

Longarm did not know what Johnson had been shooting at, but the bullet did not come near enough for him to hear its passage.

He did, however, know where his own next shot would be going.

He took time to aim, then fired square into Sam Johnson's chest.

The storekeeper became suddenly pale. He coughed once then sagged down face-first onto the floor.

Longarm considered putting a third round into the circle of pale, bald flesh that was so nicely outlined on the top of Johnson's head. After all, it presented a perfect target.

He decided against that as being unnecessary. If Johnson was not already dead, he damned soon would be.

Longarm stood, careful to keep a crate between his knees and Johnson's body, just in case the man was still alive and could see underneath the cloud of drifting gunsmoke that filled the room.

When the smoke dissipated and he could see again, Longarm approached Johnson's lifeless body. Only then did he reload his Colt and return it to the leather.

Longarm grunted. It seemed that Bert was doing a land office embalming business lately. Now he had one more body to bury.

Longarm walked out into the store and recoiled, his hand streaking to the grips of his Colt once more.

"Easy, Marshal," Eli Cruikshank said. "I heard the shooting. Thought I might be able to help."

"You can help, Eli, but not with your guns. You can go tell your Basques that the war is over with. There ain't gonna be no shooting war in McConnell County."

Cruikshank grinned. "That's apt to put me out of a job, you know."

"There's always gonna be work for a man o' your talents," Longarm said.

"It would have been interesting, though, to find out if I could have taken you," Cruikshank said.

"Care to try me now?"

Eli shook his head and smiled. "No, I think not. Perhaps someday, if we find ourselves on opposite sides of something. But not now. Not without being paid for it."

"That makes me feel just ever so much better, Eli," Longarm said with an answering smile. He had every confidence that he could have taken Cruikshank had it come to that.

And very likely Eli felt exactly the same.

Hopefully they would never find out who was right.

Longarm touched the brim of his hat, and Eli stepped respectfully aside when Custis went out to find Bert and tell him that he had another customer in the late Samuel Johnson's back room.

Watch for

LONGARM AND THE GRAND CANYON MURDERS

the 399th novel in the exciting LONGARM
series from Jove

Coming in February!